What's Susan's Secret?

An American Farce

by
Michael Parker
and
Susan Parker

A SAMUEL FRENCH ACTING EDITION

SAMUEL FRENCH

FOUNDED 1830

NEW YORK HOLLYWOOD LONDON TORONTO

SAMUELFRENCH.COM

ISBN 978-0-573-69961-0   Printed in U.S.A.   #29861

MUSIC USE NOTE

Licensees are solely responsible for obtaining formal written permission from copyright owners to use copyrighted music in the performance of this play and are strongly cautioned to do so. If no such permission is obtained by the licensee, then the licensee must use only original music that the licensee owns and controls. Licensees are solely responsible and liable for all music clearances and shall indemnify the copyright owners of the play and their licensing agent, Samuel French, Inc., against any costs, expenses, losses and liabilities arising from the use of music by licensees.

IMPORTANT BILLING AND CREDIT
REQUIREMENTS

All producers of *WHAT IS SUSAN'S SECRET?* *must* give credit to the Author of the Play in all programs distributed in connection with performances of the Play, and in all instances in which the title of the Play appears for the purposes of advertising, publicizing or otherwise exploiting the Play and/or a production. The name of the Author *must* appear on a separate line on which no other name appears, immediately following the title and *must* appear in size of type not less than fifty percent of the size of the title type.

WHAT IS SUSAN'S SECRET? was first produced by Rocky and Claudie Varcoe at Class Act Dinner Theatre in Whitby, Ontario, Canada on January 15, 2011. The performance was directed by Glenn Ottaway, with sets by Jim Renshaw. The cast was as follows:

MICHAEL....................................... Jim Renshaw
SUSAN .... Alexandra Savage-Ferr
JEAN/JULIE/BERTHA .... Linda Chapman
LARRY/BILL/MURRAY .... Graham Gauthier
JENNY/PENNY/KELLY .... Mireille Awad-Arnberg
BOBBY/JEFFREY/PAUL .... Rob Notman

CHARACTERS

MICHAEL – *(age 70-plus)* He and his wife, Susan, are the owners of a somewhat run down country inn. There are times when he appears to be totally "with it," but often wanders off into worlds of fantasy. One day he might be at The Alamo with Davy Crocket, and the next with George Washington at Valley Forge. He is often confused about names, dates, places etc. but is, however, a very endearing character with whom audiences should empathize. He is always kind, gentle, and loving towards Susan and, in the end, almost turns this play into a love story.

(Very elderly, somewhat infirm, and might best be described as "An old man with a twinkle in his eye.")

SUSAN – *(age 70-plus)* Spry and active, she appears to run The Cider Mill Inn, and is the driving force behind the "con jobs" she and Michael pull on their unsuspecting guests. She consistently forgets Michael's name, and engages him in hilarious conversations in which she and Michael are rarely "on the same page." Her attitude toward Michael, and the love and rapport they clearly share is central to the core of the plot. Whether her secret is, in fact, revealed at the end of the play is something about which the authors remain silent, preferring to let the audience be the judge.

(Hard working, efficient, competent, gentle and caring to Michael.)

JEAN – *(age 35-55)* While Jean is an interfering "busybody," her heart is in the right place. When she intervenes in the marital problems of Bobby and Jenny, it is out of genuine concern for them. She totally dominates her mild mannered husband Larry, and we are left with the impression she dominates everything and everyone around her. Things have to be done "Her Way."

(Forceful, purposeful, single-minded.)

LARRY – *(age 40-60)* A mild mannered, easy-going sort of guy, who has learned, over the years, to just go along with Jean and not make any waves. However, when Jean gets herself into a situation from which she cannot escape, he does not attempt to extricate her, but rather, in a kindly sort of way, sits back and seems to enjoy a laugh at her expense. Perhaps, in his life with Jean, there have been too few opportunities to do this.

(Long-suffering, hard-working, a devilish sense of humor.)

BOBBY – *(age 25-30)* A pleasant young man, who gets caught up in the emotional ups and downs of his new bride, Jenny. He acquiesces, perhaps a little too easily, to the fact that he has been conned by Michael and Susan, but that is probably his nature. Clearly very much in love with Jenny, he is willing to apologize when he has no idea what it is he is supposed to have done.

(Clean cut, hard working, easy-going.)

JENNY – *(age 20-25)* Young and pretty, but perhaps not too bright. She works herself into an emotional upheaval for the most trivial of reasons. Anyone, other than her gentle, easy-going husband, would probably feel like smacking her. To be kind, she is very young and on her honeymoon, and who knows what is going on in her mind.

(Immature, naïve, but in the end showing a good sense of humor.)

BILL – *(age 40-60)* Bill is a suave, sophisticated man about town. He is a reviewer for a publication, *Country Inns of America*, visiting The Cider Mill Inn incognito. While married, he has arranged a weekend tryst with his girlfriend Julie. He discovers that Michael and Susan are simply con artists and is prepared to expose them, but ethics are not his strong suit, and he compromises his principles to keep his affair secret.

(A polished, well-dressed, educated adulterer.)

JEFFREY – *(age 25-30)* If there was an award for "The Most Boring Man on the Planet," Jeffrey would win hands down. When his long suffering wife, Penny, says he's had charisma bypass surgery, we could easily believe her. He goes on and on about the stupidest subjects imaginable, blissfully unaware that he is driving everyone around him crazy. He is so boring that audiences almost like him.

(Sincere, lives in his own world.)

PENNY – *(age 20-30)* Penny seems to be driven to drink by her boring husband Jeffrey. She must never appear to be drunk or her sparkling wit and terrific sense of humor will be lost. A little tipsy, most of the time, she brings lightheartedness and laughter into the scenes with Jeffrey, to counterbalance his boring personality.

(Pretty, clearly enjoys life, funny, flighty, giggly.)

JULIE – *(age 35-45)* Julie has a libido that never lets up. She leaves the audience in no doubt as to why she is at the inn for the weekend. She is, however, sophisticated not cheap or tawdry.

(Beautiful, sensuous, single-minded.)

KELLY – *(age 20-30)* Kelly is clearly the dominant one in her relationship with Paul. She has concocted the scheme for Paul to pose as his brother Patrick so they can get the tradesmen's discount. She next comes up with the idea for him to then become her girlfriend "Pauline." She is a schemer who never gives up, constantly creating explanations for the most improbable circumstances.

(Clever, manipulative, quick-thinking.)

PAUL – *(age 25-30)* Paul is clearly under the influence of his girlfriend Kelly, She seems to be able to persuade him to do almost anything. Much against his better judgement she has him weave a tapestry of lies and deceit. He never really gets "with the program" as he alternates between the characters of Paul, his brother Patrick, and Kelly's girlfriend Pauline.

(Not very forceful, but eager to please Kelly.)

MURRAY – *(age 40-60)* Murray is a very unusual clergyman. He almost belongs in the "Hippie" generation. He arrives on a Harley wearing black leather, and using expressions like "rock on." He is, nevertheless, a genuine pastor with concern and kindness for those around him, and shows great understanding and compassion, for "Pauline" whom he believes (thanks to Kelly's manipulations) is a painfully shy claustrophobic.

(Kind, sincere, adventuresome.)

BERTHA – *(age 40-45)* Michael's sister is referred to by him as "Boot Camp Bertha." A retired army officer, she certainly lives up to that name. She is a strong comedic character, who seems to dominate the stage whenever she appears. However, prompted by Murray, she finally shows a gentler, more human side to her nature.

(Loud, domineering, aggressive.)

SETTING

The Cider Mill Inn. Somewhere U.S.A.

ACT I Sc 1: Mid-summer afternoon
ACT I Sc 2: One week later
Act II: One week later

TIME

The Present

AUTHORS' NOTES

The play is written for three-to-seven females and three-to-seven males. The characters of Michael and Susan are constant and appear in all three scenes. There are two other couples in each scene, one generally young (say, 20-30) and the other older, perhaps (50-60). So the cast could be any number between 6 and 14, depending on casting availability and how much doubling the director wanted. If doubling, attention should be given to the characters so there is enough difference in dress and manner to change appearances as much as possible for the audience.

ACT I

Scene One

(It is a late summer afternoon in a run down country inn, somewhere, U.S.A. It is very rustic and shabby looking. The front entrance is downstage right. The reception area is upstage right. This should be a counter with a call bell on it, and cluttered with papers. Behind the reception area is a door leading to the office. The whole width of the upstage area is a raised platform with open railings leading off both left and right. This platform has an open area in the center with one or two steps. There is one door to the right (room 5), one door to the left (room 6), and one door directly in the center, the bathroom. Downstage left is a field stone fireplace with a rocking chair just above it. On the left wall above the fireplace is a door to a large closet. Downstage center is a couch with a coffee table in front of it, with a vase of slightly wilted flowers, and some magazines on it.)

(As the curtain rises we see **MICHAEL** *dozing in the rocking chair by the fireplace. He is seventy-ish, moves slowly and might appear to be somewhat senile. He is wearing blue jean overalls, a checkered shirt and work boots.)*

*(***SUSAN*** enters from the office and starts to straighten up the papers on the counter. She is also seventy-ish, but spry and active. She is wearing a below the knee, old fashioned skirt, blouse, and flat shoes.)*

SUSAN. Michael, it's almost four o'clock and we have two couples checking in today. Don't you pretend to be asleep. I need you to help get this place ready.

MICHAEL. *(eyes still closed)* Watch the left flank. They're coming up from the river.

SUSAN. *(crosses left)* Oh Lordy! It's Saturday and he's at the Alamo with Davy Crockett again. *(gently takes his hands in hers)* When you're finished dealing with the Mexicans dear, I need you to help me here, at The Cider Mill Inn.

MICHAEL. Right Davy, I've got 'em in my sights. Pow! *(opens his eyes and looks at* **SUSAN***)* Gladys, what are you doing at the Alamo?

SUSAN. I'm not Gladys. Gladys was your mother. I'm Susan, your wife.

MICHAEL. No, no. Gladys was married to Robert.

SUSAN. That's right, Robert.

MICHAEL. So, I'm married to Gladys.

SUSAN. No dear, you're married to me, Susan.

MICHAEL. No, no, Susan is married to Michael, and you just called me Robert, so I'm married to Gladys.

SUSAN. That would be impossible. You can't be married to your mother.

MICHAEL. Then why did you call me Robert?

SUSAN. I didn't call you Robert.

MICHAEL. Yes, you did.

SUSAN. You can't remember what I called you, you can't remember anything. You can't even remember what you had for breakfast.

MICHAEL. I can so.

SUSAN. Alright then, what did you have for breakfast?

MICHAEL. *(thinks for a second)* Oatmeal.

SUSAN. You hate oatmeal. You haven't had oatmeal for twenty years.

MICHAEL. I didn't say it was today's breakfast.

SUSAN. *(gives him a kiss on the head)* Now that you're back among the living, did you buy the rest of the supplies for the week? It's Plumber's and Tile Layer's specials week.

MICHAEL. All taken care of.

SUSAN. Well, the new toilet was delivered a little while ago. It's sitting by the front door and we need to move it before our guests arrive.

MICHAEL. *(moves upstage to the closet and takes out a little flat dolly on wheels)* OK, I'll go get it. *(crosses right and exits front entrance as the phone rings)*

SUSAN. *(crosses right and answers the phone)* Hello, the Cider Mill Inn. Yes, you've read the ad correctly. It is the handyman's special weekend rate. This weekend only, we're discounting our rooms at ninety per cent off for Plumbers and Tile Layers, including a free dinner every night. No, I'm sorry, this weekend's rates are only for Plumbers and Tile Layers. Keep watching our ads, you never know when we'll run another handyman's special.

MICHAEL. *(enters from the front entrance straddling the toilet, which is on a small dolly, and riding it like a horse)* Hi Ho Silver, away.

SUSAN. *(watching)* What are you doing?

MICHAEL. *(stops)* You didn't expect me to carry it did you?

SUSAN. Of course not. It's just that we don't have time for your foolishness. We have guests arriving any minute.

MICHAEL. *(turns around on the toilet)* Do you remember that broken toilet on our honeymoon in Niagara Falls?

SUSAN. I've never been to Niagara Falls.

MICHAEL. You didn't go on our honeymoon?

SUSAN. Of course I went on our honeymoon, it just wasn't in Niagara Falls. You went to Niagara Falls with your sister.

MICHAEL. I went on our honeymoon with my sister?

SUSAN. Oh Martin, you're hopeless you can't remember anything about our honeymoon.

MICHAEL. I remember my name is Michael not Martin.

SUSAN. Whatever are you talking about?

MICHAEL. You just called me Martin.

SUSAN. I did not.

MICHAEL. Then who is Martin?

SUSAN. I don't know.

MICHAEL. Well, you ought to. You went on a honeymoon with him. Now who's foolish?

SUSAN. Michael, you look like King Tut on his throne. Please put the toilet in the closet before our guests arrive. *(exits to the office)*

MICHAEL. *(riding the toilet towards the closet)* A fiery horse with the speed of light, a cloud of dust and a hearty "Hi-Ho-Silver" The lone ranger rides again!

(He rides the toilet into the closet and closes the door behind him, as **JEAN** *and* **LARRY** *enter from the front entranceway.* **JEAN**, *age 50-plus, is wearing a modest sweater and matching, skirt or pants. She is carrying a purse.* **LARRY**, *age 50-plus, is wearing khaki pants and a short sleeve shirt.* **JEAN** *is a friendly busybody who is perhaps a little domineering.* **LARRY** *is quiet, distant and sometimes abrupt, but will do anything to make* **JEAN** *happy.)*

JEAN. *(glances around the room)* Oh my! Larry, I hope this place is OK. *(whispers)* It looks a little run down, don't you think?

LARRY. With ninety percent off for Plumbers, and a free dinner every night, the price sure is right. Although why they would give plumbers a discount I can't figure out. Anyway, we're here now so let's make the best of it.

JEAN. *(crosses to the fireplace)* It is romantic out here in the woods. I feel like we're on our second honeymoon.

LARRY. *(moves to the reception counter and rings the bell)* That's my girl.

*(***JEAN** *moves upstage to the closet and opens the door. She closes the door, then quickly opens it again then closes it. She hurries right to* **LARRY**.*)*

JEAN. *(whispers)* Larry, there's a man in that closet sitting on a toilet.

LARRY. You mean it's a bathroom?

JEAN. No, it's a broom closest.

SUSAN. *(enters from the office)* Good afternoon and welcome to The Cider Mill Inn. I am Susan Edwards. Can I help you?

LARRY. Yes, we're the Hamptons.

(JEAN is tugging on LARRY's shirt and nodding toward the closet.)

I'm Larry and this is my wife Jean.

SUSAN. Welcome, *(pauses and watches JEAN)* are you alright Mrs. Hampton?

JEAN. Yes. I'm perfectly alright.

SUSAN. Well then, let's get you checked in. Do you have verification that you're a plumber?

JEAN. Do you want him to bend over?

LARRY. *(gives JEAN a look)* Will my union card be sufficient? *(hands her the card)*

SUSAN. Perfect, *(hands it back to him)* if you would just fill in this form we'll get you into your room. *(hands him a pink form)* I'm sure you'll like it, it has a little private porch, and you'll be able to see quite a lot of wildlife.

(While LARRY begins to fill in the form, JEAN wanders casually over to the fireplace, looks to see that no one is watching her, quickly moves to the closet and peeks in, closes the door and crosses right She tugs on LARRY's shirt again, whispers in his ear while smiling at SUSAN.)

LARRY. Excuse me, but my wife seems to think there is a man sitting on a toilet in your broom closet.

SUSAN. Oh yes, that would be my husband, Matthew. Please excuse me for a moment.

(She crosses left to the closet, and opens the door as MICHAEL appears in the doorway. He has a long-handled toilet plunger held like a rifle on his left shoulder, and a small bucket on his head with the handle as a chin strap He marches out, paces like a soldier on sentry duty, does an about face and returns to the closet.)

SUSAN. *(cont.)* Oh Lordy! He's on sentry duty at Buckingham Palace again. *(closes the door and crosses right to the reception desk)*

JEAN. Is he alright?

SUSAN. He's fine. He just has a very active imagination. Would you mind bringing your own bags in? It's best not to disturb him when he's on sentry duty. He tends to take his responsibilities very seriously, and can get a little feisty if he's disturbed.

LARRY. No problem. Jean, would you just finish signing us in and I'll be right back. *(exits front door)*

JEAN. *(quickly signs and returns the form to* **SUSAN***)* Here you are.

SUSAN. Would you please sign this section at the bottom as well, please? *(hands the form back to* **JEAN** *who signs it and hands it back)* Well, it looks like everything is in order. *(separates the duplicate form and hands it back to* **JEAN***)*

JEAN. Are you sure your husband's alright in that closet? How long will he stay there?

SUSAN. Don't you worry about Michael, he tends to wander off a bit sometimes.

JEAN. Michael, who's Michael?

SUSAN. That's my husband.

JEAN. I thought your husband was Matthew?

SUSAN. Why ever would you think that?

JEAN. I thought I heard you....oh never mind. But I am curious as to why there is a toilet in your broom closet.

SUSAN. It's a new one. We're installing it in the main bathroom tomorrow morning.

(Enter **LARRY** *from the front door carrying two overnight bags. He moves upstage to the counter.)*

JEAN. Well, isn't that nice. *(turns to* **LARRY***)* Thank you dear, we're all checked in.

LARRY.*(puts the bags down)* Oh, by the way Mrs. Edwards, I was wondering if there are any hiking trails around here? Something, you know, not too strenuous.

(JEAN *cannot resist the temptation to investigate* MICHAEL *in the closet again. She shuffles left.*)

SUSAN. Absolutely. We have a little sketch map somewhere. Give me a second. *(exit to the office)*

JEAN. *(now at the closet, opens the door and peers in, then takes a step or two towards* LARRY*)* Larry, he's still marching up and down in the closet.

LARRY. Just leave him be dear.

SUSAN. *(enters from the office with a small map)* Here it is.

(As LARRY *turns right to* SUSAN, MICHAEL *appears in the closet doorway, places the plunger firmly on* JEAN*'s derriere and pulls her into the closet.*)

There are three trails and they all start...

(JEAN *steps into the room, the plunger still attached to her rear.* SUSAN *has her head down looking at the map, and so does not see* JEAN *who opens her mouth to say something but* MICHAEL *pulls her back into the closet.*)

...right at the end of the driveway.

LARRY. Thank you, may I keep the map?

SUSAN. Let me just make a copy for you. *(exit to the office)*

JEAN. *(enters from the closet now free of the plunger, and stands just outside the closet door)* Larry, do something!

LARRY. What are you talking about?

JEAN. It's Mr. Edwards.

LARRY. I told you, just leave him be.

JEAN. No, no, you don't understand.

LARRY. I understand that Mrs. Edwards told us not to disturb her husband.

SUSAN. *(enters from the office with the map copy)* Here you are.

LARRY. Thank you.

(He turns right as MICHAEL *re-appears with the plunger, attaches it firmly to* JEAN*'s derriere and pulls her back into the closet.* LARRY *takes the map and turns left but* JEAN *is once again in the closet.*)

Jean! Leave him alone.

SUSAN. *(hurries over to the closet)* Oh dear, I hope she's alright. He doesn't like intruders at Buckingham Palace.

(She goes into the closet and immediately re-appears with a somewhat flustered JEAN. *They leave the closet door open and cross right.)*

I'm so sorry, Mrs. Hampton, he does get carried away a little bit sometimes.

LARRY. I told you not to go in the closet.

JEAN. Like I had a choice.

SUSAN. *(now again behind the counter, hands* JEAN *a room key)* You're in room five, right up the landing there.

LARRY. *(picks up the bags and moves towards room five)* I'm looking forward to a nice dinner tonight and sleeping late tomorrow morning.

JEAN. Me too.

SUSAN. You won't be sleeping too late, I hope. You need to be finished with your work by twelve noon.

LARRY. *(stops dead in his tracks and turns downstage)* Work?

SUSAN. Yes, you've agreed to install our new toilet.

LARRY. I have done no such thing.

SUSAN. Well, technically you haven't, but your wife signed the contract on your behalf.

LARRY. Contract?

SUSAN. Yes, it's all in paragraphs five, six and seven.

LARRY. *(takes the check in form copy out of* JEAN*'s hands and looks at it)* Jean, what did you sign?

JEAN. Just the check in form.

LARRY. This is a work contract.

JEAN. Well, nobody ever reads the small print.

LARRY. Well, I'm just not going to do it.

SUSAN. I see, then you need to read paragraph eight.

LARRY. *(frowns and looks at* SUSAN*)* Why don't you just tell me what's in paragraph eight.

SUSAN. If you don't do the work agreed to in paragraphs five six and seven, then we charge you on your credit card for a whole week at full rates, *(She is busy with a hand held calculator.)* and that would total one thousand seven hundred and forty-two dollars.*

JEAN. That's outrageous. You can't get away with that.

SUSAN. I'm afraid we can. You signed and authorized us to debit your card. The lawyers charged us a fortune. This contract is very legal and very binding.

LARRY. *(turns to* **JEAN***)* What have you got us into?

JEAN. Well, it's not that bad, I mean, you're a plumber after all. You've installed hundreds of toilets. It won't take that much time. Besides we're staying here practically free, and we get dinner. All in all, I think I've done a pretty good job.

LARRY. Well, can I at least sleep in tomorrow and do it in the afternoon?

SUSAN. I'm afraid not, we've already planned to re-tile the entire bathroom in the afternoon.

MICHAEL. *(enters from the closet and crosses right)* So, are you our plumber?

LARRY. It looks that way.

JEAN. I'm glad to see you're off duty now.

MICHAEL. What are you talking about? Is your wife feeling alright?

LARRY. She's fine.

MICHAEL. Well, the toilet's in the closet, and any tools you'll need are right there too. See you at dinner. *(crosses to counter)*

LARRY. *(picks up the luggage and heads up to room five with* **JEAN** *following)* I can't believe this.

JEAN. It really wasn't my fault. You'd need a magnifying glass to read all that stuff. *(They exit to bedroom five.)*

MICHAEL. *(leans across the counter and gives* **SUSAN** *a kiss on the cheek)* Well dear, we did it again.

---

*This dollar amount may be changed at the director's discretion based on the current market in the area, but should be an amount which is ridiculous in nature.

SUSAN. Yep, worked like a charm. They were easy. They didn't give us any hassle at all. *(We hear a car pull up.)* Well, that will be our Tile Layer. Michael, why don't you check on the dinner menus and make sure they are ready for tonight. **(MICHAEL** *exits to the office.)*

(Enter from the front entrance **BOBBY**, *carrying a suitcase, followed by* **JENNY**. *They are on their honeymoon.* **BOBBY** *is thirty-ish, wearing black jeans, tennis shoes, and a T-shirt. He is a clean cut young man, very much in love with his young bride.* **JENNY** *is in her mid-twenties, wearing a casual skirt, blouse or top, mid-heeled sandals and a matching purse. She is extremely pretty but appears to be somewhat upset. She is quietly sobbing into a handkerchief. They move up to the counter.)*

SUSAN. Welcome to the Cider Mill Inn, I'm Susan Edwards. You must be Mr. and Mrs. Brader.

BOBBY. Yes, we are. I'm Bobby and this is my new bride, Jenny. *(turns to* **JENNY***)* I'll get us checked in, dear. Why don't you go sit down.

(JENNY *crosses left, and sits in the rocking chair. She continues to sob.)*

SUSAN. Is Mrs. Brader all right?

BOBBY. She'll be OK. She's just a little upset.

SUSAN. *(takes out paperwork)* You'll be staying in room six which is our honeymoon suite, as you requested. However, before I can guarantee you the ninety per cent off weekend special, I do need to verify that you are an experienced Tile Layer.

BOBBY. Oh, yes, I've been doing it for years. Here's a card from my company. *(hands* **SUSAN** *the card who looks at it and hands it back)*

SUSAN. Wonderful, now if you'll just sign here.

(hands a pink form and pen to **BOBBY** *who signs it)*

Oh, you need to sign here as well.

(BOBBY *signs again and returns the form and pen.)*

Excellent. You're in room six, right up the stairs there.

(detaches the duplicate copy and hands keys and the duplicate to **BOBBY***)*

SUSAN. *(cont.)* Now, tomorrow you —

(There's a loud nose blowing raspberry into her handkerchief from **JENNY** *and* **BOBBY** *hurries over to her side.)*

Is Mrs. Brader alright?

BOBBY. She'll be fine. She just needs to rest a little.

SUSAN. Would you like my husband to help you with your bag?

BOBBY. No, that's alright, I've got it.

SUSAN. Dinner's usually about six thirty and my husband will have the menu out here shortly. If you need anything, please ring the bell.

(She gives the bell a ring, and **MICHAEL** *enters immediately to answer it.* **SUSAN** *just gives him "a look." Without breaking stride he wheels about and exits.)*

We're right here in the office. *(exits to the office)*

BOBBY. *(crosses right to pick up the suitcase)* I'm really not sure why you're so upset, dear, but if you just come to our room, we can talk about it.

JENNY. I'd rather just sit out here for a few minutes if you don't mind.

BOBBY. O.K, if you really want to. I'll go unpack and wait for you. *(exits to room six)*

*(***JENNY*** watches* **BOBBY** *enter the bedroom then bursts into tears. Enter* **JEAN** *from room five. She notices* **JENNY** *in the rocker and moves downstage towards her.)*

JEAN. I'm sorry. I couldn't help but see that you're upset. Are you alright?

JENNY. Not really.

JEAN. Is there anything I can do? I'm Jean, by the way. *(shakes hands with* **JENNY***)*

JENNY. *(shakes hands)* I'm Jenny.

JEAN. *(sits on the couch, left arm)* I'm a great listener.

JENNY. Would you mind if I asked you something?

JEAN. Not at all.

JENNY. Are you married?

JEAN. Yes.

JENNY. Has your husband ever asked you to do something you didn't want to do?

JEAN. I suppose so yes. Why don't you tell me what it is that's got you all upset like this.

JENNY. Well, we're on our honeymoon, and last night at three in the morning my husband made an unreasonable demand.

JEAN. At three in the morning? Oh, the brute! You poor girl.

JENNY. I thought I knew Bobby better than that, but now...I don't know. I think my marriage is over before it's begun. I don't know what to do? I'm not even sure I want to be alone with him.

JEAN. Don't you worry about a thing. Why don't you come and lie down in our room, and I'll get my husband Larry to have a talk with Bobby.

JENNY. Oh, I can't do that.

JEAN. *(stands and pulls JENNY along with her to the door of room five)* Of course you can, Larry won't mind at all. I'm sure he will talk some sense into your husband and he'll apologize. *(She opens the door to room five.)* Larry, I need you out here for a moment please.

LARRY. *(comes to the door)* What is it? I was just about to lie down.

JEAN. You can do that later. Larry, this is Jenny, she's going to rest in our room. *(turns to JENNY)* You go lie down dear and don't worry about anything. Larry will take care of this. *(pushes JENNY inside and closes the door)*

LARRY. Larry will take care of what? Why is a strange woman lying in our bed where I'm supposed to be right now? I don't like that look in your eye, Jean.

JEAN. All you have to do is go next door to room six and explain to her husband why it is wrong to make an unreasonable demand on that poor young girl at three in the morning on their honeymoon.

LARRY. What?

JEAN. Well, Jenny and Bobby are on their honeymoon, and last night, at three o'clock in the morning, he made an unreasonable demand on her. She is so distraught and thinks her marriage is over. I'm sure you can make him see that what he did was wrong. Make him apologize, and they can get on with their honeymoon.

LARRY. Why me? Why not you?

JEAN. Because.

LARRY. Because?

JEAN. Well, because...because he needs a man-to-man talk.

LARRY. You expect me to knock on a perfect stranger's door and tell him he needs to apologize to his wife, for something that's none of our business anyway?

JEAN. Yes, and don't forget the part about three in the morning. *(gives him a kiss and exits to bedroom five)*

LARRY. *(stands in the hallway facing downstage muttering softly to himself, imitating* **JEAN***)* "I'm sure you can make him see what he did was wrong. Make him apologize. Then they can get on with their honeymoon..."

*(**MICHAEL** enters from the office walking backwards slowly. He moves left till he is clear of the counter, then he mimics stepping off a ladder.)*

MICHAEL. One small step for man, one giant leap for mankind.

LARRY. Come in Houston, we have a problem.

MICHAEL. *(now back to normal)* Really, can I help?

LARRY. Help with what?

MICHAEL. Your problem.

LARRY. I don't have a problem.

MICHAEL. You said you did.

LARRY. Well, I don't.

MICHAEL. Oh, OK.

*(**SUSAN** enters from the office.)*

SUSAN. Michael, where did you put the menu? Oh, hello, Mr. Hampton. Everything all right?

LARRY. As alright as possible given the circumstances, I suppose.

*(Enter **BOBBY** from room six.)*

SUSAN. Wonderful! Oh hello, Mr. Brader. Have you met Mr. Hampton?

BOBBY. *(comes downstage and shakes hands with **LARRY**)* Hello.

SUSAN. *(to **MICHAEL**)* Did you finish writing out the menu Mitchell?

MICHAEL. No, but Michael did.

SUSAN. *(exits to office with **MICHAEL** following)* Well, who else would? Sometimes you just don't make any sense.

MICHAEL. You're telling me I'm the one who doesn't make sense?

BOBBY. You haven't seen my wife, have you? I left her sitting in that rocking chair.

LARRY. Well, as a matter of fact, I have. She's in our room.

BOBBY. What is she doing in your room?

LARRY. Actually, I have no idea. You see my wife...wait a minute, can we sit down?

*(They sit on the couch, **LARRY** left, **BOBBY** right.)*

You see my wife has this strange idea, – first I should tell you that my wife has strange ideas all the time. She asked me to talk to you, I want you to know this is not my idea, I don't think it's any of our business. But when Jean gets an idea into her head it's best to go along with it. So, there it is.

BOBBY. No disrespect, Mr. Hampton, but I haven't a clue what you're talking about.

LARRY. Oh boy! Sometimes it's just best to come straight out with it. Here it is. Your wife told my wife that you made an unreasonable demand on her at three in the morning.

BOBBY. And that's what has her so upset?

LARRY. Apparently so.

BOBBY. I didn't think it was unreasonable, she'd already got out of bed to go to the bathroom.

LARRY. She'd already got – wait a minute. Exactly what demand did you make?

BOBBY. I wouldn't call it a demand. I just asked her if she would mind opening the window. I was hot.

LARRY. And that's it?

BOBBY. Yes, do you think that's unreasonable, Mr. Hampton?

*(**LARRY** shakes his head no and begins to laugh.)*

What's so funny?

LARRY. Well, Jean thinks that….oh never mind. *(moves upstage to room five)* Let's get our wives out here and get this sorted out.

*(knocks on the door and **JEAN** appears)*

Jean, could you and Jenny come out here please.

JEAN. *(enters followed by **JENNY**)* Good job, Larry. I knew you could do it.

*(moves downstage followed by **JENNY** and **LARRY**)*

So young man, are you ready to apologize?

JENNY. Yes, Bobby, I'd like an apology.

BOBBY. But I didn't do anything wrong, did I, Mr. Hampton?

LARRY. I'm staying out of this one.

JENNY. Didn't do anything wrong? How can you think that it's OK to make a demand like that…

JEAN. At three in the morning? Young man, I can't believe–

LARRY. *(grabs **JEAN** by the arm and pulls her aside)* Jean, this is between the two of them.

JEAN. But –

LARRY. You need to let them sort this out. It's not what you think.

JENNY. I'm not your slave, I'm your wife.

JEAN. That's the spirit.

JENNY. My mother always told me that big things start in little ways. One little demand here, becomes a lifetime of demanding, and she told me never to let it get started, and Mrs. Hampton agrees. Three o'clock in the morning is not a reasonable time to ask me to do anything. I wouldn't ask you to do anything at three in the morning.

BOBBY. If it were the other way around, I wouldn't have minded.

JEAN. Of course you wouldn't, you're a male.

JENNY. There, you see, you just don't understand. I thought you were more sensitive than this.

BOBBY. I really didn't think it was a big deal.

JEAN. Big deal!...Big deal!....Larry, do something!

LARRY. I don't think it's a big deal either.

JEAN. Larry Hampton, I can't believe what I'm hearing. Jenny, let's go.

(JEAN & JENNY *start to move upstage.*)

BOBBY. No wait a minute. If it's so important to you, I apologize. I swear I will never ask you to open a window at three in the morning ever again.

(*There is a long pause.*)

JEAN. Open a window?

LARRY. (*grins at* JEAN) Open a window.

JENNY. Oh, Bobby. (*runs into* BOBBY*'s arms and kisses him*)

JEAN. Well, how was I to know....I mean the poor girl was so upset...I was only trying to help...besides...you didn't do anything to help the situation either.

JENNY. I was being so silly. I love you. (*kisses* BOBBY)

BOBBY. Me too, you! Listen, we're on our honeymoon and have the whole weekend together, so let's start over.

LARRY. They appear to be happy now, so let's let it go at that.

JENNY. *(giggling)* And you were so smart to find us this place for practically nothing. *(kisses him again)*

LARRY. Wait a minute, did you say practically nothing? You wouldn't happen to be here on the tradesman's special would you?

JENNY. How did you know?

LARRY. Did you sign in already?

JENNY. Yes, we did.

JEAN. Did you read the fine print?

BOBBY. No

LARRY. What's your line of work?

BOBBY. I'm a Tile Layer.

LARRY. Then they didn't tell you?

JENNY. Tell us what?

JEAN. That you probably signed a work contract to tile the bathroom tomorrow afternoon. Larry, I think you'd better explain to Bobby how he's been conned.

LARRY. Do you have your check-in form?

BOBBY. It's in our room.

LARRY. Why don't we go look at it.

(**BOBBY** *exits to room six followed by* **LARRY**.)

JENNY. This is my honeymoon.

JEAN. *(sits on the couch left)* I know dear, but it's not so bad. As you said, it's costing you practically nothing, and you do get a free dinner.

(*Enter* **SUSAN** *from the office with a menu. She stops behind the counter.*)

JENNY. *(moves to the counter)* Is it true you had us sign a work contract to do some tiling?

SUSAN. It's just a very small bathroom. Please tell your husband he will be expected to start work at noon tomorrow. The tiles are in the closet as well as any tools and materials he may need.

JENNY. That's not fair. It's my honeymoon.

SUSAN. Well, you can always pay full price for the room.

JEAN. You don't want to do that. Cheer up. We can go for a walk or something while he's working.

JENNY. Do you have the dinner menu?

SUSAN. Yes, it's right here. *(hands* JENNY *the menu)*

JENNY. Well, dinner had better make-up for your trickery.

SUSAN. I'm sure you'll find the menu very interesting. Just ring the bell when you're ready to place your order for tonight.

(She gives the bell a ring and MICHAEL *enters immediately to answer it.* SUSAN *just gives him "a look." Without breaking stride he wheels about and exits, followed by* SUSAN.*)*

*(*JENNY *comes downstage and sits on the couch right end, as* BOBBY *and* LARRY *enter from room 6 and move downstage.)*

BOBBY. How could I be so stupid? I wondered why there was a duplicate copy.

LARRY. Cheer up, at least you get to sleep in, I have to be at work at nine. *(sits in the rocker)*

BOBBY. *(gives* JENNY *a kiss on the cheek and sits on the right arm on the couch)* I'm afraid I'm going to have to do a little work tomorrow afternoon dear. I'm sorry.

JENNY. It's OK. Jean said she'll keep me company.

JEAN. Well at least we get a free dinner. Jenny, what's on the menu?

JENNY. *(reads for a moment and makes a face)* Earthworm soup?

JEAN. *(grabs the menu)* Squirrel Tail Tidbits?

LARRY. *(grabs the menu)* Possum Pie?

BOBBY. *(Strides over and grabs the menu, reading as he returns to the couch right arm.)* Breast of Turkey Buzzard, and if you're still hungry, Buffalo Chip Cookies.

(There is a long silence as LARRY *goes to the counter and rings the bell.)*

SUSAN. *(immediately enters)* What can I do for you?

LARRY. Mrs. Edwards, we've been discussing your dinner menu, and we all agree that perhaps it might be nice to eat out tonight. Is there a restaurant nearby that you could recommend?

SUSAN. As a matter of fact, there is a charming little place right down the road about a half a mile away. I'd be happy to make reservations for you.

LARRY. Thank you, six o'clock would be fine. Come on Jean, let's go take a quick nap. Who knows, I might just make an unreasonable demand on you!

JEAN. *(giggling)* Oh, Larry! *(Both exit to room five.)*

BOBBY. *(looks at* **JENNY***)* What do you say, Jenny?

JENNY. *(giggling, pulls* **BOBBY** *up and leads him upstage)* Just don't ask me to open the window. *(exit to room six)*

SUSAN. *(dials the phone)* Hello, Brookside restaurant? This is Susan at The Cider Mill Inn. I need a reservation for four at six this evening. Yes, the usual table. Yes our usual twenty percent commission would be fine. Thank you.

MICHAEL. *(enters from the office)* Are they going out for dinner?

SUSAN. Oh yes.

MICHAEL. Good, what are we having?

SUSAN. Well, French onion soup, sirloin tips, fresh asparagus with hollandaise sauce, and your favorite, baked Alaska.

*(curtain)**

---

*Depending on the "Curtain Down" time required by the director, there may just be time for Michael and Susan to change into a different shirt and blouse.

Scene Two
One week later

(The setting is exactly the same as Act I.)

(As the curtain rises we see **MICHAEL** *dozing in the rocking chair by the fireplace.* **SUSAN** *enters from the office with a large bundle of towels. They are dressed the same as Scene One.)*

SUSAN. *(crosses left to* **MICHAEL***)* Michael, our guests will be arriving any moment. Have you got everything ready?

MICHAEL. *(eyes still closed)* We've got to find more wood.

SUSAN. We have plenty of wood. It was delivered yesterday for our new deck.

MICHAEL. *(eyes still closed)* We almost had a cave-in in section seven.

SUSAN. *(sets the towels down on the couch, and gently takes his hands in hers)* Lordy! I forgot. It's Friday, he's tunneling out of Stalag seventeen again. Michael dear, *(* **MICHAEL** *opens his eyes)* our guests will be arriving soon, and I haven't quite finished getting room five ready. I need you to hold down the fort.

MICHAEL. *(stands up and salutes)* Ja wohl, Herr General.* Martha, you can't be here, there are no women allowed in Stalag seventeen.

SUSAN. I'm not Martha, I'm Susan, and you're not in Stalag seventeen.

MICHAEL. Are you sure you're not Martha?

SUSAN. Oh Morgan, of course I'm sure. Martha was your first wife.

MICHAEL. Morgan was married to Martha?

SUSAN. No dear, you were married to Martha.

MICHAEL. Then who was Morgan married to?

SUSAN. How should I know?

MICHAEL. Well, do you know who you're married to?

---

* The word "general" is pronounced in German with a hard "G."

SUSAN. Yes dear, you.

MICHAEL. Well you can't be married to me, I'm married to Martha.

SUSAN. *(gives him a kiss on the head)* That was a long time ago. You're married to me and have been for a long time.

MICHAEL. I'm so glad, dear. I'd choose you every day of the week and twice on Sunday.

SUSAN. That's sweet dear, but now that you're back at the Cider Mill Inn, I just want to remind you that we have three parties checking in today. Mr. and Mrs. Woodson, they're here on the tradesman special. He's the carpenter here to build our new deck. There is a Mr. Herman and a Ms. Monroe, who are just regular guests. If they check-in before I'm finished in room five, please make sure you give Mr. Herman and Ms. Monroe the yellow forms, and Mr. and Mrs. Woodson get the tradesman special pink form. We wouldn't want them to get the wrong forms now would we, dear?

MICHAEL. Right.

SUSAN. *(picks up the towels and moves upstage to room five)* And Michael, stay out of Stalag seventeen while I'm gone.

MICHAEL. *(salutes)* Ja wohl, Herr General.

SUSAN. Michael! *(exits to room five)*

MICHAEL. Right, dear. *(Immediately he drops to his hands and knees and begins to crawl across the floor towards the closet.)*

(BILL enters from the front entrance. As we will see later, it is important that BILL has a mustache. He is wearing an oversized pair of black rimmed glasses, long sleeve white shirt, dress pants, and loafers. He carries a small overnight bag. He watches MICHAEL, who is half way across the room.)

BILL. Excuse me!

MICHAEL. *(Raises his head, yelling out as he bumps it on the ceiling of the imaginary tunnel. When he reaches the closet he stands up.)* Yep, the tunnel has just enough headroom.

(Turns and sees **BILL**, *and is immediately normal. He then crosses right to behind the counter as* **BILL** *moves upstage from the entrance to the counter.)*

MICHAEL. *(cont.)* Oh hello, welcome to The Cider Mill Inn. I'm Michael Edwards. May I help you sir?

BILL. I don't know, – er – are you alright?

MICHAEL. I'm perfectly fine, thank you. What can I do for you?

BILL. I'm Bill Herman. I have a reservation.

MICHAEL. Right, if you would just fill in this form. *(grabs a pink form from behind the counter and hands it to* **BILL***)*

BILL. You sure have a pretty spot here in the hills. What a great place for a weekend escape.

MICHAEL. *(eyes bulging)* ESCAPE!

(Immediately drops to his knees and crawls left to the closet. **BILL** *watches as* **SUSAN** *enters from room five with a smaller pile of towels.* **MICHAEL** *exits to the closet and closes the door.)*

SUSAN. *(comes downstage behind the counter, and puts the towels down)* Oh Lordy! He's still in Stalag seventeen. Hi, I'm Susan Edwards.

BILL. Hello, I'm Bill Herman.

SUSAN. Please excuse my husband.

BILL. That's alright. Though I have to admit, he did take me by surprise.

SUSAN. He's quite harmless. He just has an overactive imagination, and I see he gave you the wrong form. *(snatches the pink one away and replaces it with a yellow form)*

BILL. Wrong form?

SUSAN. Oh it's nothing. That was one of the old ones. We don't use those anymore.

BILL. I see. *(begins to fill out the form)* I must say you have a beautiful place here.

SUSAN. Thank you. We think so too.

BILL. How long have you owned it?

SUSAN. Over twenty years, but we only opened it as an inn about five years ago.

BILL. *(hands the form to* **SUSAN***)* Here you are.

SUSAN. I must apologize, your room isn't quite ready. If you'd like to make yourself comfortable over by the fire, I just need a few more minutes.

BILL. That's fine, take your time.

(Crosses left with his luggage and sits in the rocking chair as **SUSAN** *picks up the towels and exits to room six.* **BILL** *looks around and then takes a small recorder out of his pocket as* **MICHAEL***, unseen by* **BILL***, opens the closet door and watches.* **BILL** *speaks into the recorder.)*

Country Inns of America. Rating report on the Cider Mill Inn, on *[INSERT CURRENT DATE]*, by your traveling critic Bill Herman. Check in 4 pm. Reception quite unusual. Mr. Edwards does not appear to be dealing with a full deck. *(***MICHAEL** *reacts.)* However, Mrs. Edwards is very pleasant and efficient. *(***MICHAEL** *reacts.)* Arrived early, room not quite ready. Décor rustic and a little run down, but that might just be its charm. Certainly the setting and location live up to its reputation.

*(***SUSAN** *enters from room six, crosses right to behind the desk, as* **BILL** *hurriedly stands up and slips the recorder into his pocket. He turns upstage as* **MICHAEL** *closes the door.)*

SUSAN. Thank you for waiting, Mr. Herman. Your room is all ready. It's room six. *(hands him a key)* If you need anything I'll be right here in the office, just ring the bell. *(exits to the office)*

BILL. Thank you, I'm sure I'll be just fine. *(picks up his luggage and exits to room six)*

(Enter JEFFREY and PENNY from the front entrance. JEFFREY is 30-ish wearing a tan polo shirt, brown pants and brown shoes. He carries two small suitcases. He is, as we shall see, the world's greatest bore. He talks incessantly about subjects in which no one has any interest. PENNY, his long suffering wife is 30-ish, attractive, wearing a sundress, sandals, and purse, with a small flask inside. She is carrying a glass, filled with a clear liquid. She is never drunk, but seems to be driven to drink by her boring husband. She always appears to be just a little bit tipsy, never really drunk, and perhaps flighty and giggly.)

JEFFREY. Oh my! Penny, did you see that yellow pine by the front door? Did you know that yellow pine isn't really yellow, it's called yellow pine to distinguish it from white pine, which of course isn't really white, but the grain of yellow pine gives it an appearance of yellow when the sun hits it. The grain of white pine doesn't really make it look white at all. I've often wondered if there was such a thing as a grey pine would the grain of the grey pine make it look grey or simply not grey at all but another color altogether.

(PENNY takes out the flask out of her purse and pours some into her glass.)

When sunshine hits the yellow pine it does tend to look yellow, but only when the sun hits it. I wonder if that would be the case for grey pine, if there was any grey pine, which as far as I know there isn't.

PENNY. Congress doesn't take this long.

(rings the call bell and SUSAN enters immediately)

Thank God, a real human being.

SUSAN. May I help you?

PENNY. Yes, do you have a muzzle?

SUSAN. I beg your pardon?

JEFFREY. Hello, we're the Woodson's.

SUSAN. Ah yes, you're here on the carpenter's special this weekend.

(Places a pink form on the counter, as **PENNY** *wanders left waving her glass in the air.)*

Please complete this form.

JEFFREY. *(writing)* Don't you find it interesting that my last name is Woodson and I'm actually in the business of working with wood. I remember when I was just a young boy my father, whose name was also Woodson...

PENNY. *(almost to herself)* No kidding.

JEFFREY. *(doesn't miss a beat)* ...gave me my first piece of wood when I was only two years old. I got it for Christmas, or was it my birthday...anyway, it was a lovely piece of pine wood. Did you know that pine grows in warm climates as well as northern ones? Well, I treasured that piece of pine for years, I had it when I went to elementary school, middle school, high school and college, but then, when I got married it disappeared. *(hands the form to* **SUSAN***)*

PENNY. *(again to herself)* I burned it.

SUSAN. Well, I can see that you're our carpenter. You'll be in room five. *(hands him the key)*

MICHAEL. *(Comes out of the closest, crosses quickly right to the counter, sees the pink form which* **JEFFREY** *has just signed and grabs it from* **SUSAN***.)* Susan dear, I think we've given him the wrong colored form here.

SUSAN. *(grabs the form back from* **MICHAEL***)* These are the Woodson's and they're here on the tradesman's special.

MICHAEL. *(grabs the form back from* **SUSAN***)* I don't think we have a tradesman's special running this weekend dear.

SUSAN. *(grabs the form back from* **MICHAEL***)* Of course we do. I don't know what has got into you. Please just go and get the drawing of the new deck that Mr. Woodson is going to build for us tomorrow.

MICHAEL. There's something you need to know.

SUSAN. Just get the drawings would you please.

MICHAEL. *(shrugs his shoulders and exits to the office)* OK.

JEFFREY. What did you just say?

SUSAN. *(hands him the duplicate copy)* What you just signed is a work contract. You just agreed to lay the new deck for us tomorrow. (**JEFFREY** *opens his mouth to speak.)* Please read paragraphs five, six, seven and eight.

PENNY. *(moves right)* You mean he has to work tomorrow?

SUSAN. I'm afraid so.

PENNY. Oh, thank God. I thought I was going to have to spend the whole weekend cooped up with him. He has the intellectual capacity of a tuna sandwich.

SUSAN. I'm so glad, you like our arrangement.

PENNY. He's going to ask you a question in a minute.

JEFFREY. *(studying the pink form)* Paragraph five is a bit ambiguous. It reminds me of a contract I once made with my father. It might seem strange to you for someone to have a contract with their own father, but I found it very satisfactory. He seemed to think that every one should have an allotted time for speaking, and so he made me sign this contract. He had certain times for speaking and I had certain times. If he spoke in one of my allotted times there was a penalty. I can't remember what the penalty was because I can't remember him ever speaking in my time. I, on the other hand, if I spoke in his time, had my next speaking time reduced. It was all in the contract.

PENNY. I should have taken out a contract on you years ago.

SUSAN. *(to **PENNY**)* Does he always talk like that?

PENNY. Ever since he had charisma bypass surgery.

SUSAN. Do you have a question Mr. Woodson?

JEFFREY. What? Oh yes. Just what would that total be in paragraph eight if I don't do the work?

SUSAN. *(picks up her calculator)* Charged to your credit card, for a whole week at full rates, that would be one thousand seven hundred and forty two dollars.

JEFFREY. This was supposed to be a special weekend with my adoring wife, but I can't afford that.

PENNY. Thank God.

JEFFREY. But I don't have any tools or anything.

SUSAN. All the tools you'll need are in the closet over there.

PENNY. He won't need a drill...he can simply "bore" anything. *(giggles)*

JEFFREY. Penny dear, how can you be so beautiful and drink so much?

PENNY. God made me beautiful so you would be attracted to me. I drink so much so I can be attracted to you.

JEFFREY. Don't you find me exciting dear?

PENNY. On a scale of one to ten, NO.

JEFFREY. *(picks up luggage and heads to room five followed by* **PENNY***)* I'm sorry about this, dear. I really hadn't planned on it, but it won't be all that bad, I'm sure you'll be able to find some way to entertain yourself while I'm working. Perhaps you would like to count how many hairs there are in your hairbrush? Or another favorite of mine is to pick a tree, my favorite of course are pines, and count the number of branches, then the number of pine cones, and.... *(exits to bedroom five)*

MICHAEL. *(comes out of the office with the plans, and hands them to her)* You have no idea what you've just done. There is a spy in our midst.

SUSAN. *(sets the plans under the counter)* Michael, for heaven's sake, get out of Stalag Seventeen.

MICHAEL. *(pacing around and looking towards room six)* No, no, no... it's Mr. Herman. He's a critic for *Country Inns of America*. I overheard him dictating notes when I was in the closet. He appears to be writing a review of The Cider Mill Inn.

SUSAN. Are you sure?

MICHAEL. Of course I'm sure, I heard him.

SUSAN. Wow! *Country Inns of America.* That's a nationally recognized magazine. A review in there could make or break us. That's terrific.

MICHAEL. Until he finds out about the tradesman's special. You've got to get rid of the Woodsons.

SUSAN. It's too late, they've already signed. Don't worry, it'll work out. Just give me a minute to think. I know, we'll just make sure they don't meet. You make sure that there is only one copy of the menu for Mr. & Mrs. Woodson, and take a complimentary bottle of wine to Mr. Herman's room. Keep your eyes open, and try to make sure the Woodsons don't talk to him.

MICHAEL. *(sits in the rocker)* I suppose that will work. You know, this reminds me of the time we were staying in a cabin, and there was a burglar.

SUSAN. *(crosses left and sits on the couch)* Oh Michael, you're hopeless, we never stayed in a cabin with a burglar.

MICHAEL. We did too.

SUSAN. All right then, where were we?

MICHAEL. Yosemite.

SUSAN. We've never been to Yosemite together. I went there once with my first husband, Murray.

MICHAEL. Murray was a burglar?

SUSAN. Of course not.

MICHAEL. So you shared a cabin with Murray and a burglar?

SUSAN. I stayed with Murray. Can't you get it Marvin, there was no burglar.

MICHAEL. Ah ha! Marvin was the burglar.

SUSAN. Who's Marvin?

MICHAEL. The burglar wasn't he?

SUSAN. I don't know dear. Can we get back to the menu.

MICHAEL. Did you know he was a burglar when you married him?

SUSAN. Of course not, because he wasn't a burglar.

MICHAEL. But he was in your bed.

SUSAN. Who was?

MICHAEL. The burglar.

SUSAN. There was a burglar in my bed?

MICHAEL. Sounds like the title of a play. Of course there was.

SUSAN. How do you figure that one?

MICHAEL. Elementary, my dear Watson.

SUSAN. Oh, Lordy! He's about to become Sherlock Holmes again. Michael can you please stay out of Baker Street and take care of the menu, and Mr. Herman's wine?

MICHAEL. Ah, the mystery of the missing wine.

SUSAN. Michael!

MICHAEL. Alright dear. *(exits to the office)*

(Enter JULIE *from the front entrance. She is age 40-50, but doesn't look her age. She is sensuous, flirtatious and attractive. She is wearing a low cut summer outfit, complete with matching high heel shoes, hat, large sun glasses, jewelry, and purse. She carries a small overnight case.)*

SUSAN. *(sees* JULIE *and crosses right)* Hello, I'm Susan Edwards. Welcome to the Cider Mill Inn can I help you? *(goes behind the counter)*

JULIE. Hello, I'm Julie Monroe, I have a reservation.

SUSAN. Of course, Ms. Monroe. If you would just complete this. *(hands her a yellow form, which* JULIE *begins to fill in)* May I ask how you found us?

JULIE. Oh…well…a friend told me about this place and said it would be perfect for a little get away. *(hands the form back to* SUSAN*)*

SUSAN. *(hands her a key)* You'll be in room four, up the steps and down the hallway to the left.

JULIE. Thank you.

SUSAN. If you need anything, I'll be right here in the office, just ring the bell.

(She gives the bell a ring and **MICHAEL** *enters immediately to answer it.* **SUSAN** *just gives him "a look."
Without breaking stride he wheels about and exits to the
office, followed by* **SUSAN**, *as* **BILL** *enters from room six.)*

*(***BILL** *and* **JULIE** *see each other, look around to make
sure they are alone, then rush together and embrace at
the foot of the steps.)*

BILL. My darling Julie.

JULIE. Our weekend together at last. *(kisses him passionately
on the lips)*

BILL. *(pulls away and looks around)* We must be very discreet.
I'm here on a working weekend, all expenses paid, to
do a write-up on this place. *(They head upstage to room
six.)*

JULIE. All right, I'll let you out of bed for fifteen minutes
every hour. *(They embrace again just outside the door of
room six.)* Now, just let me go slip into something more
suitable.

(Enter **MICHAEL** *from the office. He is now wearing
an overcoat, a deer stalker hat, a calabash pipe in his
mouth, and carrying a magnifying glass.* **JULIE** *quickly
pushes* **BILL** *into room six and closes the door. She
watches as* **MICHAEL** *creeps around the room looking at
things through his magnifying glass. She moves right on
the landing to the steps as* **MICHAEL** *sees her.)*

MICHAEL. You are exposed!

JULIE. *(looks down at herself)* I am?

MICHAEL. This is the curious case of the affair at the Cider
Mill Inn.

JULIE. *(comes downstage a few steps)* My affair is none of your
business.

MICHAEL. When a crime has been committed it is always
my business.

JULIE. What crime? What are you talking about?

MICHAEL. Aha, I see that you are left handed.

JULIE. No, I'm not.

MICHAEL. Then I deduce that you are right handed.

JULIE. Is that a crime?

MICHAEL. Come now, don't bandy words with me. I shall strip you of your outer coverings and expose you to the world.

JULIE. You'll do no such thing.

MICHAEL. Layer by layer the real you will be revealed.

JULIE. It most certainly will not.

MICHAEL. I have deduced what lies underneath and all shall be bared.

JULIE. What's underneath is none of your business and nothing shall be bared.

MICHAEL. When you have eliminated the impossible, whatever remains, however improbable, must be the truth. You will not be able to hide from me. Now madam, I must go to investigate the curious incident of the dog in the night. *(exit to the office)*

JULIE. *(Rushes upstage to room six and pounds on the door.* **BILL** *enters.)* Bill, I'm not sure it's safe to stay here.

BILL. Of course it is, no one knows about us.

JULIE. I'm not so sure, I just met this crazy old man who accused me of having an affair.

BILL. Oh, that would be Mr. Edwards. He's OK.

JULIE. But he said he wanted to strip me and reveal my underwear.

BILL. Whoa, are you sure?

JULIE. He said I would be exposed and naked.

BILL. Well, his wife says he's harmless, but if what you say is true, this is going to be one of the most interesting reviews I've ever written. Don't worry, I'll make sure you're safe.

JULIE. Well, just so long as I don't have to be alone with him. *(runs her hands through his hair)* However, there is someone here I'd like to be alone with. *(kisses* **BILL***)*

*(Enter **JEFFREY** and **PENNY** from room five. **BILL** and **JULIE** quickly separate.)*

JEFFREY. Hello. I'm Jeffrey, and this is my lovely bride of many years, Penny. *(**PENNY** rolls her eyes.)*

BILL. Hi, I'm Bill Herman.

JULIE. Hello, I'm Julie Monroe.

PENNY. Hi, maybe we can all meet up later and have a drink.

JULIE. That would be nice, but I have a feeling I'm going to be very busy. *(looks at **BILL**)*

JEFFREY. Mr. Herman, may I have a word with you?

BILL. Of course.

PENNY. A word? A single word? Oh, you are moments away from a bad experience.

*(During this speech, everybody backs slowly away. **PENNY** to the bathroom, **BILL** to room six and **JULIE**, who takes her suitcase, goes off right to room four. **JULIE** and **BILL** make signs to each other to meet up.)*

JEFFREY. You know, I can't help but admire your mustache. I've been thinking about starting one while I was here. I was looking in the mirror this morning and it seemed that I had more hairs on the right side than I did on the left. So, I asked myself, I said "Self, why would there be more hairs on one side than the other?" Then I started to count them, and it was absolutely fascinating. Do you know I counted seven hundred and twenty four on the left side. Then I got to thinking why seven hundred and twenty four? Why an even number?

*(**MICHAEL** enters from the office with a bottle of wine, and a glass on a tray. Sees **JEFFREY** and backs slowly off.)*

Would I have an even number of the right side? Then I thought, do new ones start growing all the time or are they always the same old ones? What do you think Mr. Herman, should I grow one? *(stops talking and looks around, but everyone is gone)* Oh! Now what? I know. I can count the number of leaves on the ground compared to the number still on that tree by the front door. *(exits the front entrance)*

(MICHAEL enters from the office with a bottle of wine and a glass on a tray and heads up to room 6 as PENNY comes out of the bathroom. She takes the bottle of wine and glass off the tray, and exits to room 5, leaving MICHAEL standing there with the empty tray.)

SUSAN. *(enters from the office)* Michael, did you ever get that wine to Mr. Herman's room?

MICHAEL. Almost.

SUSAN. Almost?

MICHAEL. Almost.

SUSAN. Well then, I take it that's a no?

MICHAEL. Yes.

SUSAN. Then please make it a yes and deliver the wine to Mr. Herman. We need to make a good impression on him. And while you're at it you can deliver tonight's menu to the Woodsons.

(MICHAEL exits to the office as JEFFREY enters from the front entrance, sees SUSAN and moves to the counter.)

JEFFREY. Hello Mrs. Edwards, what a beautiful evening. I went out to look at the wood and I noticed your amazing lawn. It's very thick and luscious. I was wondering how often you water it and the type of fertilizer you use? It appears that you seem to have more blades of grass to a square inch in your yard compared to the grass in mine. I only water my yard once a week and use a generic brand of fertilizer...

SUSAN. Please excuse me Mr. Woodson, I need to help my husband. *(quickly exits to the office)*

JEFFREY. I know, I can count how many blades per square inch. *(quickly exits front entrance)*

(JULIE enters from upstage right, pauses, looks around, sees no one, and hurries to room six. Prior to knocking, she turns to see if anyone is observing her. MICHAEL

enters with a menu in one hand and a tray with a wine bottle and a glass in the other. **JULIE** *sees* **MICHAEL**, *turns quickly and exits to the bathroom.* **MICHAEL** *heads up to* **PENNY**'s *room and knocks on the door.* **PENNY** *opens the door.* **MICHAEL** *is standing to the left of the door of room five. The menu is in his right hand and the tray in his left. As* **PENNY** *opens the door he hands her the menu, which she takes in her left hand, then reaches with her right hand and takes the wine bottle off the tray.)*

PENNY. Thank you, how nice. *(She closes the door, leaving the tray with the wine glass in* **MICHAEL**'s *hand.)*

*(**MICHAEL** shrugs and comes downstage. He places the tray on the counter and exits to the office.* **JULIE** *enters from the bathroom, looks around, sees no one, and knocks on the door of room six.* **BILL** *opens the door and* **JULIE** *throws herself into his arms and kisses him full on the lips as* **MICHAEL** *enters with another bottle of wine. He sees them and ducks behind the counter.)*

JULIE. Let's get this weekend started. *(Gives him a kiss on the lips and then pulls him into the room and closes the door.)*

*(**MICHAEL** stands up, still holding the bottle of wine, and moves left staring at the door of room six as* **SUSAN** *enters from the office.)*

SUSAN. Michael, haven't you delivered the wine yet?

MICHAEL. Not exactly. *(He turns and comes back right as* **SUSAN** *stays behind the counter.)* Listen, Mr. Herman and Ms. Monroe are an item. They're here for a weekend together.

SUSAN. Well it's none of our business. The important thing is that he doesn't find out about the work contracts.

(Enter **JEFFREY** *from the front entrance.* **MICHAEL** *and* **SUSAN** *see him coming and run into the office to avoid him as* **BILL** *and* **JULIE** *enter from room 6.)*

JULIE. *(gives* **BILL** *a kiss)* Just give me a few minutes to slip into something more comfortable. Oh, hello Mr. Woodson.

JEFFREY. Hello

BILL. Hello. Enjoying your evening?

JEFFREY. Not really. The pine wood they've bought for the new deck is beautiful, and I will enjoy working with it, but I'm not happy about having to work on what was supposed to be a vacation.

(**JULIE** *and* **BILL** *come downstage.*)

BILL. What do you mean?

JEFFREY. Well, when I checked in on the tradesman special, I thought it was a regular check-in form, but it turns out it was a work contract.

JULIE. A work contract?

JEFFREY. Yes, in order to receive the discounted rate, I have to build them a new deck. If not, I have to pay for a whole week at full rates, which I can't afford.

JULIE. That's not fair.

BILL. That's what the different check in forms were all about. What a con. What a story. Wait a minute. Let's sit down for a minute. I need to make some notes.

(**BILL** *sits in the rocker and takes out his recorder,* **JULIE** *sits on the couch left side,* **JEFFREY** *sits couch right side.*)

(**PENNY** *Enters from room five with the menu. Comes downstage and sits on the right arm of the couch.*)

PENNY. Jeffrey, just wait till you see this menu. It's a hoot. Literally. Owl soup…

(*She tries to read the menu, but breaks down into a fit of giggles.* **JEFFREY** *takes the menu.*)

JULIE. (*looking at the menu which* **JEFFREY** *is now holding*) Owl soup! Armadillo on the half shell! Rack of raccoon! Oh and listen to this, stuffed garlic roasted hedgehog. This is awful.

BILL. Wait till *Country Inns of America* reads this menu.

JEFFREY. So much for our free dinner.

BILL. Dinner will be on me. (*moves to the desk and rings the bell*) Just let me handle this situation. I think I've got Mrs. Edwards' number.

(**SUSAN** *enters from the office.*)

BILL. *(cont.)* Mrs. Edwards, we've decided we'd like to go out for dinner tonight, perhaps you could recommend a restaurant.

SUSAN. Absolutely, would you like me to make reservations for you?

BILL. Thank you. That would be nice. By the way, how long have you been offering these so-called free dinners?

SUSAN. So-called?

BILL. Oh, come now Mrs. Edwards. How many of these dinners have you actually cooked for anyone?

SUSAN. Well, it takes a discriminating taste to enjoy our menu.

BILL. It most certainly does. I'm sure my readers will be interested in your menus.

SUSAN. Readers, Mr. Herman?

BILL. Yes, readers. I'm a reviewer for *Country Inns of America.*

SUSAN. I take it then, Mr. Herman, that you do not plan to write a favorable review?

BILL. I intend to write the truth, Mrs. Edwards.

SUSAN. The truth? What would that be?

BILL. That you and your husband are nothing more or less than con-artists preying on unsuspecting guests.

SUSAN. I'm sure your wife would be interested to learn the truth.

BILL. My wife?

SUSAN. Yes, your wife. She called a few minutes ago and wanted to know if you arrived here safely. I told her you had and I would tell you that she'd called. You might be interested to know that I chose not to reveal the truth to her about your affair with Ms. Monroe. So Mr. Herman, would you agree that sometimes the truth is better left untold?

BILL. Are you adding blackmail to your list of accomplishments, Mrs. Edwards?

SUSAN. Oh dear, that is such an ugly word, Mr. Herman. Could we use a different one? Perhaps "Cooperation?" Now, I'll be happy to make reservations, and in return I'm sure you'll find a way to write a glowing review of The Cider Mill Inn.

BILL. Alright Mrs. Edwards, you win. Make the reservations.

(MICHAEL enters from the office with another bottle of wine on a tray. He comes left as PENNY, jumps to her feet, crosses right and grabs it.)

PENNY. I like this place, Jeffrey, the wine never stops flowing. Come on, we've got an hour before dinner. Let's make the most of it. *(exit to room five)*

JULIE. A whole hour, the mind boggles. Come on lover boy. *(drags BILL to room six)*

(MICHAEL and SUSAN give each other a high five.)

SUSAN. I love you, Martin.

MICHAEL. I love you, Sally.

(curtain)

ACT II

Several weeks later.

(The setting is exactly the same as Act I, with the addition of a basket of balloons on the counter.)

*(As the curtain rises we see **MICHAEL** dozing in the rocking chair by the fireplace. He is wearing the same clothes as in Act I, but with a different shirt. **SUSAN** enters from the front entrance. She is wearing a plain dress, flat shoes, and is carrying a large cardboard box.)*

SUSAN. *(crosses left to the closet)* Michael, the new lights have arrived for the deck. Just in time for our electrician's tradesman special this weekend. Can you get the closet door for me?

MICHAEL. Camp five, come in camp five. We need sixteen oxygen tanks at camp six and we need them immediately.

SUSAN. *(places box on the floor by the closet door and comes downstage)* Oh Lordy! He's half way up Everest again.

MICHAEL. If the weather turns before we're on the South Col, we're all in trouble.

SUSAN. Michael, you're going to be in trouble if you don't get down off that mountain! We have guests checking in shortly and I need help.

MICHAEL. *(opens his eyes)* Beatrice, what in heaven's name are you doing on Everest dressed like that? You're going to freeze to death. Put some clothes on, girl.

SUSAN. *(gently takes his hands in hers)* I'm all right dear. I'm not Beatrice. Beatrice was my sister, and your sister-in-law. I'm Susan, and I'm not freezing to death.

MICHAEL. You mean we left Beatrice on Everest?

SUSAN. I'm quite sure Beatrice has never been to Everest.

MICHAEL. Yes, she has. I was there with her last week. We need to mount an expedition to rescue her.

SUSAN. Michael, that's impossible.

MICHAEL. No, its not. Rescue teams are always available to help on Everest.

SUSAN. No dear, what I meant was, Beatrice died two years ago.

MICHAEL. There you see, I told you she'd freeze to death. We shouldn't have left her on Everest.

SUSAN. Michael, please come down off the mountain. Mr. and Mrs. Harding will be arriving any minute now. They're on the tradesman special. He's the electrician who will hopefully install the lights on the new deck. Now just help me get this box in the closet.

MICHAEL. *(stands up and sighs)* OK, OK, I'll bet you Sir Edmund Hillary's wife never asked him to put boxes in closets. *(picks up the box as* SUSAN *opens the closet door)* I still don't know why they put the breaker box in this closet and how anyone is supposed to know which of the breakers are for the deck.

SUSAN. Oh, Mitchell, he's an electrician. It's his job to know how to do these things.

MICHAEL. So the electricians name is Mitchell? I thought you said it was Harding.

SUSAN. It is.

MICHAEL. Then is Mitchell his first name?

SUSAN. Who?

MICHAEL. The electrician.

SUSAN. How should I know, they registered as Mr. and Mrs. Harding. I don't know where you came up with the name Mitchell.

MICHAEL. From you, you said, "Mitchell, he's an electrician."

SUSAN. I did not. I said, "Michael, he's an electrician."

MICHAEL. I am?

SUSAN. No dear you're not, that's why we're having Mr. Harding do the lights. *(crosses right towards the office followed by* **MICHAEL***)* The last time you tried to do something electrical, *[INSERT THE NAME OF THE NEAREST MAJOR CITY]* had a black out. There are no other guests checked in, so all you have to do is take care of the menu.

(The phone rings and **MICHAEL** *picks it up.)*

MICHAEL. Hello.

SUSAN. I wish you'd let me answer the phones.

MICHAEL. *(hangs up)* OK.

SUSAN. I didn't want you to hang up.

MICHAEL. *(picks up the phone)* They're gone. *(He hangs up and the phone and it immediately rings again.)*

SUSAN. *(picks up the phone)* Good afternoon, Cider Mill Inn. *(pauses)* It's for you. *(hands* **MICHAEL** *the phone)*

MICHAEL. *(listens for a second or two then turns to* **SUSAN***)* It's a telemarketer.

SUSAN. Just hang up.

MICHAEL. But you told me….

SUSAN. Hang up, Michael.

MICHAEL. *(hangs up the phone)* OK, but I wish you'd make up your mind.

SUSAN. By the way Michael, what are these balloons doing here?

MICHAEL. They're for your birthday.

SUSAN. My birthday isn't for three months.

MICHAEL. I thought it was today.

SUSAN. No, dear.

MICHAEL Then whose birthday is it today?

SUSAN. I'm sure I don't know.

MICHAEL. Well, it has to be someone's.

SUSAN. I'm sure it is dear.

MICHAEL. Maybe it was Gladys's.

SUSAN. Michael, please, let's not go down that road. Why don't you just do the menu dear.

MICHAEL. I have a great one planned this time. *(exits to the office followed by* **SUSAN***)*

(Enter **PAUL HARDING** *and* **KELLY ROBERTS**. **PAUL**, *age early twenties is wearing blue jeans, a T-shirt, and tennis shoes with a baseball cap. He is fairly quiet, a "does-things by the book" type of guy. He is carrying a backpack.* **KELLY**, *early twenties, is wearing a pretty summer dress with sandals. She is carrying an overnight bag. As we shall see later, she is wearing a wig, which she will later have to share with* **PAUL**.* **KELLY** *is clever, devious, and tends to dominate* **PAUL**.*)*

KELLY. OK, Paul, now just remember, that when we check in you're not Paul Harding, but your brother Patrick because we're using his union card to get the electrician's discount.

PAUL. Kelly, I wish you hadn't talked me into doing this. It's dishonest. I'm not a very good liar you know.

KELLY. Listen, we get ninety percent off, and we get to spend the whole weekend alone together. Now that has to be worth something? *(grabs him and gives him a kiss)*

PAUL. Well, I guess you're right, as long no one asks me anything about electricity.

KELLY. Oh Paul, you're such a worrywart. Just show them the union card, we'll get the discount, and we'll have a beautiful weekend together. *(kisses him)*

MICHAEL. *(enters from the office and watches them kissing for a second or two, then, using a Bogart imitation)* "Of all the gin joints, in all the towns, in all the world, you walk into mine!"

PAUL. *(quickly separates from* **KELLY***)* I'm so sorry. We're the Hardings, we have a reservations.

---

*Depending on the length and style of Kelly's hair, the wig could merely be a hair extension.

MICHAEL. *(imitating Claude Rains' English accent)* Round up all the usual suspects.

PAUL. See Kelly, we haven't even checked in and we're already in trouble.

KELLY. Play it once Sam, for old times sake.

MICHAEL. *(Bogart's voice)* Welcome to Rick's Place.

KELLY. I just loved that movie.

MICHAEL. Me too.

PAUL. What movie?

(Enter SUSAN from the office.)

MICHAEL. *(Bogart's voice)* Here's looking at you kid!

SUSAN. Oh Lordy! Now he's in Casablanca. I'm Susan Edwards, I do apologize for my husband.

MICHAEL. I don't know what you're talking about, I'm not in Casablanca. I'm right here at the Cider Mill Inn. I was just having some fun with our guests, the Hardings.

SUSAN. *(a little deflated)* Oh, OK. Well, have you got them checked in yet?

MICHAEL. Ah! Forgot about that.

SUSAN. Oh Malcolm, you're hopeless. *(produces the pink form)* If you would just fill this in.

(PAUL begins to fill in the form.)

MICHAEL *(Bogart's voice)* "I think this is the beginning of a beautiful friendship."

KELLY. You do a wonderful Bogart impression.

SUSAN. He should, he's had years of practice. *(to PAUL)* In order to qualify for the tradesman special, I will need to see some type of identification to prove you're an electrician.

KELLY. It's in your wallet, Patrick.

PAUL. Who? *(KELLY gives him a look.)* Oh, right, *(takes out his wallet and hands the I.D. to SUSAN)* Here it is.

SUSAN. Well, everything looks in order. Just make sure you sign the bottom section as well.

PAUL. *(signs the bottom and hands the form back to* **SUSAN** *who separates the copy and gives it to* **PAUL***)* Well, that was easy enough.

SUSAN. I'm glad you think so. Mr. Harding, would you mind stepping into the office with me a minute while Malcolm shows Mrs. Harding to her room? *(hands* **MICHAEL** *the key to room six)*

PAUL. I guess not.

SUSAN. Good, I just want you to look at the plans for the lights being installed on our new deck.

PAUL. Kelly?

KELLY. I'm sure you'll be fine just looking at the plans, Patrick. I'll wait for you in the room.

SUSAN. Shall we? *(exits to the office followed by* **PAUL***)*

KELLY. What in heavens name brought you to Casablanca?

MICHAEL. *(Picks up* **KELLY***'s bag and they both head up to room six. Bogart voice.)* My health. I came to Casablanca for the waters.

KELLY. Waters? What waters? We're in the desert.

MICHAEL. *(Bogart voice)* I was misinformed. *(They both laugh.)* If you need anything don't hesitate to ask. Just ring the bell on the counter if we're not around. *(hands* **KELLY** *her bag)*

KELLY. Thanks. *(enters room six and closes the door)*

*(***MICHAEL** *turns downstage.)*

PAUL. *(offstage in the office yells)* WHAT?

MICHAEL *(stands still, grins, and says the words, while mimicking with his hands)* It's all in paragraphs five, six and seven.

PAUL. *(offstage)* NO WAY!

MICHAEL. *(says the words)* Then you need to read paragraph eight.

PAUL. *(offstage)* HOW MUCH WOULD THAT BE?

MICHAEL. *(says the words, and mimics* **SUSAN** *with the calculator)* Charged to your credit card for a full week that would be one thousand seven hundred and forty two dollars.

PAUL. *(offstage)* THAT'S OUTRAGEOUS. I CAN'T AFFORD THAT. *(storms in from the office, followed by* **SUSAN***)* I need to talk to Kelly. *(exits to room six)*

SUSAN. *(behind the counter)* That's a good idea, Mr. Harding. I'm sure she'll help you "see the light." Michael, please stop lollygagging around. I need you to finish the menu for Mr. and Mrs. Harding.

MICHAEL. Right. *(exits to the office)*

(Enter **MURRAY ROBINSON** *from the front entrance. Age 50+. He is wearing a black leather outfit and carrying a helmet.)*

SUSAN. Hello, welcome to the Cider Mill Inn, I'm Susan Edwards, may I help you?

MURRAY. *(moves left up towards counter)* I know I don't have a reservation, but I was wondering if there is any room at the inn?

SUSAN. As it happens you're in luck. We have a charming little room available, it's number five. The rate is on the form.

(Pulls out the yellow form and hands it to **MURRAY** *as he places his helmet on the counter.)*

MURRAY. Rock on! This will be fine. *(begins to fill out the form)* I love my bike, but it sure will be good to relax and stretch out for awhile.

SUSAN. How long have you been traveling?

MURRAY. Well, actually not that long, but I don't get out on the bike as often as I used to, so I tend to get a little stiff. Here you go. *(Hands the form to* **SUSAN***, then unzips his jacket revealing a clerical collar and grey shirt.)*

SUSAN. *(staring at* **MURRAY***)* Oh my goodness!

MURRAY. Something wrong Mrs. Edwards?

SUSAN. Good heavens, you're a reverend.

MURRAY. You bet your sweet bippie I am.

SUSAN. I'm sorry, I didn't mean any disrespect. I'm just not used to seeing a clergyman in black leather.

MURRAY. No reason you have to turn in your black leather for a white collar now, is there?

SUSAN. I suppose not.

MURRAY. I always say, if Jesus rode into Jerusalem today it would be on a HOG, not a donkey.

SUSAN. Hog?

MURRAY. A Harley Ms. Edwards, a Harley Davidson motorcycle.

SUSAN. Oh I see, a hog verses a donkey, very different. Right. Well, I do hope you enjoy your stay. *(hands a key to* **MURRAY***)* Room five is just up the steps. If you need anything please ring the bell.

(She gives the bell a ring and **MICHAEL** *enters immediately to answer it.* **SUSAN** *just gives him "a look." Without breaking stride he wheels about and exits to the office, followed by* **SUSAN**.*)*

MURRAY. Rock on! Well, I'll just go get my saddlebag. *(exits to the front entrance)*

(Enter **KELLY** *followed by* **PAUL** *from room six.)*

KELLY. Come on Paul, you can at least look in the closet, it can't be that hard. After all, you've helped your brother a few times.

PAUL. Sure I did, I held the tools and a flashlight for him. I didn't rewire a house.

KELLY. Now, you said the electrical box is in the closet.

PAUL. You're nuts Kelly, we're never going to get away with this.

*(***KELLY** *opens the closet door, and they both enter leaving the door open.)*

(Enter **MURRAY** *from the front entrance carrying the saddlebag. He picks up his helmet from the counter and heads towards room five, but stops short of the stairs as he hears noises from the closet.)*

Kelly, stop that. I'm supposed to be looking at the electrical box.

KELLY. I was just trying to find the light switch. Wait here a minute. *(steps out of the closet to find the switch and sees* **MURRAY***)* Reverend Robinson, what are you doing here?

MURRAY. Why I'm staying here tonight. How nice to see you, Kelly.

PAUL. Who are you talking to?

*(***KELLY*** quickly pulls the door shut, and locks the door with the key.)*

MURRAY. Are you staying here too? Are your parents here?

KELLY. Yes…no…maybe.

(Muffled noises from the closet as **PAUL** *attempts to open the door.)*

MURRAY. Is there somebody in there?

KELLY. Yes…no…maybe.

MURRAY. Maybe?

KELLY. Well, it's Paul. *(***MURRAY*** reacts to "***PAUL***.")* …I mean Pauline, it's my girlfriend Pauline.

MURRAY. Aren't you going to bring her out and introduce us?

KELLY. No…Yes…maybe. *(unlocks the closest door and sticks her head in)* Pauline, would you like to meet the Reverend Robinson. *(TOTAL SILENCE)* I didn't think so. *(turns to* **MURRAY***)* She says no.

MURRAY. Kelly, I'm not being nosy, well, yes I am, what exactly is she doing in the closet?

KELLY. Pauline is extremely shy, and when she thought she heard someone she jumped into the closest. I was simply trying to persuade her to come out again.

MURRAY. But you locked her in the closet.

KELLY. Ah, yes, well….she's also claustrophobic, and to help her get over it, she needs to be locked in a small place once a day.

MURRAY. I must say that is an unusual treatment for claustrophobia. *(calling out through the open door)* I want you to know there's nothing wrong with being shy. But when you decide to come out of the closet, I'd like to meet you. I might be able to help you with your problem.

KELLY. That's awful nice of you, Reverend, but I don't want to keep you from getting to your room.

MURRAY. Well, alright, but I hope I'll see you later. You too, Pauline. *(exits to room five)*

PAUL. *(comes out of the closet)* What the heck was that all about?

KELLY. That was the Reverend Robinson. He's the pastor at my church. He knows my whole family.

PAUL. So?

KELLY. So, I can't let him know I'm here with my boyfriend for a weekend.

PAUL. Well that solves all our problems. I'm not an electrician, and you can't be seen with me, so let's just grab our bags and go.

KELLY. You're forgetting about one thing.

PAUL. What's that?

KELLY. You signed a contract and we can't afford to break it.

PAUL. What are we going to do?

KELLY. You heard me tell the Reverend I was here with my girlfriend Pauline…

PAUL. You want me to be a girl?

KELLY. Yes

PAUL. No

KELLY. One thousand seven hundred and forty two dollars

PAUL. What am I going to wear?

KELLY. One of my dresses.

PAUL. Never. I'll never wear a dress.

KELLY. One thousand seven hundred and forty two dollars.

PAUL. What about my hair?

KELLY. *(whips off her wig and hands it to* **PAUL***)* You know this isn't my real hair.

PAUL. I can't wear that.

KELLY. One thousand seven hundred and forty two dollars.

PAUL. Then what about – *(Cups his hands over an imaginary bust.* **KELLY** *looks desperately around the room, sees the balloons on the counter, rushes over and holds up two huge balloons.)*

PAUL. That's ridiculous! *(***KELLY** *just stands there.)* I know, I know, one thousand seven hundred and forty two dollars.

KELLY. Come on, let's get you dressed...Pauline. *(starts to move upstage towards room six)*

PAUL. *(following* **KELLY***)* Kelly, this is never going to work, no ones ever going to believe I'm a girl. Mr. and Mrs. Edwards think I'm Patrick the electrician, I'm really Paul, and now you want me to be Pauline who's shy and claustrophobic. We'll never pull this off.

KELLY. Must I remind you of – *(enters room six)*

PAUL. *(follows* **KELLY** *into the room and closes the door)* I know, I know.

MICHAEL. *(Enters with a hop, skip, and a jump, carrying the menu followed by* **SUSAN***. He sits in the rocking chair waving the menu around.)* I've really outdone myself with tonight's menu this time. I should be a master chef by now.

SUSAN. *(follows to the rocking chair and stands)* Michael, you've never cooked anything in your entire life.

MICHAEL. Yes, I have.

SUSAN. What?

MICHAEL. I cooked up this idea to have a fake menu so no one would stay for dinner didn't I?

SUSAN. Yes dear, I guess you did. *(kisses him on the forehead)* You always did have a creative bent, Marcus.

MICHAEL. I'm not Marcus, Marcus was your first husband. I'm Michael.

SUSAN. Marcus wasn't my first husband, Mitchell was. Mitchell could never have thought up this idea, but Marcus could.

MICHAEL. Really?

SUSAN. Absolutely, Marcus was definitely creative.

MICHAEL. *(pauses)* Who was Marcus?

SUSAN. Marcus who?

MICHAEL. You know, the creative one.

SUSAN. Oh him. He was my old boyfriend, I left him for Mitchell.

MICHAEL. You left me for Mitchell?

SUSAN. I didn't leave you Michael, I left Marcus.

MICHAEL. Why did you leave Marcus?

SUSAN. Because I met my husband.

MICHAEL. But I'm your husband.

SUSAN. I know that dear, and I would never leave you.

MICHAEL. But you called me "Marcus".

SUSAN. Why would I do that?

MICHAEL. You must admit dear you have been known to mix up names once in a while.

SUSAN. I admit no such thing, You just get me a little confused. ·

MICHAEL. Talking about being confused, do you remember that time when we were on that cruise ship and couldn't find our cabin?

SUSAN. I've never been on a cruise ship. I get seasick.

MICHAEL. I distinctly remember wandering around looking for our cabin when a nice young man in a red baseball cap told us we were on the wrong deck.

SUSAN. That was in a hotel in Denver.

MICHAEL. The cruise ship went to Denver?

SUSAN. How could a cruise ship get to Denver?

MICHAEL. I don't know, but I distinctly remember being on a cruise ship.

SUSAN. That must have been with your first wife, Martha.

MICHAEL. No, no Martha would never go on a cruise ship, she got seasick.

SUSAN. Michael, dear, that's me. I'm the one who gets seasick.

MICHAEL. So I went on a cruise ship with Martha to Denver?

SUSAN. I'm sure you went somewhere on a cruise ship with Martha, but I can assure you it was not to Denver. You're just a little confused right now dear.

MICHAEL. That's the pot calling the kettle black.

SUSAN. Am I the pot or the kettle?

   (**MICHAEL** *opens his mouth as if to answer but is cut off by* **SUSAN**.)

   Never mind *(kisses him on the forehead)* Why don't you just read me the menu.

MICHAEL. I thought you'd never ask. For starters I've got....

   (*Enter* **MURRAY**, *from room five. He moves downstage to* **MICHAEL** *and* **SUSAN**. *He has removed the leathers and is now wearing dark pants and tennis shoes.*)

MURRAY. Hello Ms. Edwards.

SUSAN. Hello Reverend. I don't believe you've met my husband, Michael.

MICHAEL. Hello, can we do anything for you?

MURRAY. As a matter of fact, I was wondering if you serve dinner here?

MICHAEL. Of course we do.

SUSAN. *(gives him a look, snatches the menu out of* **MICHAEL**'s *hand and hides it behind her back)* My husband is quite right, however, it's a very simple menu.

MURRAY. I don't need anything fancy.

SUSAN. Well, it's a bit country style and city folk don't usually find it to their liking.

MURRAY. I dare say I'm not your usual anything, Mrs. Edwards. Do you have a menu I could look at?

MICHAEL. Sure do. It's right here.

(Grabs the menu from behind **SUSAN** *and hands it to* **MURRAY**, *while* **SUSAN** *glares at* **MICHAEL**.*)*

SUSAN. There is a charming little restaurant about a half-mile down the road I would highly recommend if you're looking for a more elaborate meal. Michael, why don't we leave the Reverend Robinson to look at the menu. Let me know if you prefer the restaurant, I'll be happy to make a reservation for you. Come along dear. *(They exit to the office.)*

MURRAY. *(glances at the menu, then does a double take and starts to chuckle)* I can't believe this.

*(**KELLY** opens the door of room six and looks around. **MURRAY** looks up and sees her and motions for her to come down. She quickly closes the door behind her and moves downstage.)*

KELLY. Hi Reverend. What can I do for you?

MURRAY. I was hoping you and Pauline would join me for dinner tonight. I thought I'd take a sneak peak at the menu. Have you seen it? It's unbelievable. *(hands* **KELLY** *the menu)*

KELLY. *(shaking her head no, starts to read the menu then gasps)* Braised mole or breast of crow? How awful. *(hands the menu back to* **MURRAY***)* No thanks.

MURRAY. Rock on! Where's your spirit of adventure. I thought the roasted toad au jus with toad stool sauce sounded interesting.

KELLY. You'd eat that stuff?

MURRAY. Nothing ventured, nothing gained. You need to broaden your horizons. Try new things. *(looks at the menu)* Far out, how about the crow's egg soufflé?

KELLY. Well, I might be willing to try that, but I have a feeling Pauline won't. I think she's at the limit for broadening her horizons this weekend.

MURRAY. Speaking of Pauline, is she going to spend the whole weekend in her room?

KELLY. No, of course not, it's just that she's so very shy. Excuse me and I'll go get her. *(enters room six leaving the door open)*

MURRAY. *(looks at the menu)* Rock on, I didn't even notice the dessert. Jellied frog spawn with wild gooseberry sauce. Ohh, even I'm not brave enough for that.

(PAUL enters from room six, now dressed as Pauline, wearing a dress with padded bosom, high heels, a little make-up and KELLY's blonde wig, pushed by KELLY as MURRAY turns to watch.)

(turns upstage and takes a step or two towards them) You must be Pauline, how nice to finally meet you.

(Extends his hand, but PAUL just stands there. KELLY who is behind PAUL, takes his right elbow and pushes it forward. PAUL and MURRAY shake hands.)

KELLY. You need to say hello, Pauline.

PAUL. *(in a high pitched voice)* Hello.

(PAUL and KELLY come downstage and sit on the couch, PAUL right, KELLY left. PAUL sits with his knees wide apart and KELLY quickly grabs one of his legs, shoves his knees together and crosses his legs for him.)

MURRAY. So, what brings you girls here this weekend?

KELLY. Well, er…er…it's part of Pauline's therapy.

PAUL. It is?

KELLY. Yes, *(elbows PAUL)* she has to go out and meet strangers.

PAUL. I do?

MURRAY. Rock on! Well, now that we've met, I hope we're not going to be strangers. Kelly and I were just looking at the menu. Perhaps we could all have dinner together?

KELLY. I'm not sure Pauline will be up for that. Can we get back to you?

MURRAY. Groovy. I was just heading out to explore the woods and build up an appetite for that interesting menu. *(winks at* **KELLY***)* See you two later. *(exits front entrance)*

PAUL. Kelly, Pauline is definitely not up to having dinner with anybody. How long do I have to wear this ridiculous outfit? I can't even walk in these stupid shoes. *(attempts to walk but wobbles off)* And even if I could, my feet are killing me. There's no way we can keep this up. Let's just get out of here.

KELLY. One thousand *(***PAUL*** joins in)* seven hundred and forty two dollars.

MICHAEL. *(Enters from the kitchen,* **KELLY** *sees him coming and quickly pushes* **PAUL** *into the closet.)* Hello there, everything alright? Who's that in the closet?

KELLY. Oh, that's Paul – er – I mean Patrick. I'm just waiting for him to er…um…check out the electrical box to make sure that…well….that everything checks out.

MICHAEL. Right, well I'm just getting some wood for the fireplace, then I'll be happy to help him.

KELLY. That's very kind, but I'm sure he can handle it himself.

PAUL. *(from inside the closet)* I can?

KELLY. Yes, you can.

MICHAEL. Well it's no problem for me to lend a helping hand. I enjoy working with electricity. I'll be right back. *(exit to the front entrance)*

PAUL. *(steps out of the closet)* Kelly, he can't see me like this… do something!

KELLY. Right, wait just a minute.

(She dashes up to bedroom six. **PAUL** *looks down at what he is wearing and them does a few muscle man poses, as* **KELLY** *returns with a pair of pants, shirt and shoes.)*

What are you doing?

PAUL. What does it look like I'm doing? I'm a man, pretending to be a woman, pretending to be a man.

(MICHAEL enters from the front entrance carrying an armful of wood. KELLY grabs PAUL and they both enter the closet.)

MICHAEL. Okay men, all we've got left is green wood. Let's try to get a fire going so we can keep our spirits up. Temperatures are dropping quickly and it looks like more snow's a-comin'.

(MICHAEL drops to his knees in the middle of the stage and begins to build a log fire. SUSAN. Enters from the office and comes quickly downstage.)

Ah, there you are Martha, can you lend a hand please?

SUSAN. What are you doing? Michael, what day is it today?

MICHAEL. It's January 17, 1778, and it's starting to snow. Now, would you please help? The men are getting cold.

SUSAN. Oh Lordy! He's George Washington at Valley Forge again. *(SUSAN drops down to her knees and takes MICHAEL's hands.)* George dear, we already have a fire going.

MICHAEL. Oh thank you, Martha. I knew I could count on you.

SUSAN. Please dear, I'm not Martha, I'm Susan.

MICHAEL. What happened to Martha?

SUSAN. That depends, are you George or Michael?

MICHAEL. *(now back in reality)* You've been married to me all these years and you still don't know my name?

SUSAN. *(kisses the top of his head)* Of course I do dear. Now, why don't you just put the wood in the bin. By the way, have you seen Mr. Harding?

MICHAEL. *(picks up the wood and starts to put it in the bin)* Yep, he's in the closet checking the electrical box.

SUSAN. *(helps pick up the wood)* Oh, good. He's going to do the work then. I thought perhaps he was going to give us trouble.

MICHAEL. I've offered to lend him a hand.

SUSAN. *(horrified)* Michael, I expressly forbid you to go any-where near that electrical box.

MICHAEL. But....

SUSAN. Michael!

MICHAEL. I really could…

SUSAN. No

MICHAEL. But…

SUSAN. No!

MICHAEL. OK dear. You know, you sounded just like my sister when she….

SUSAN. Ah, speaking of your sister, she's arriving today.

MICHAEL. *(there is a long pause then in a whisper)* Which one?

SUSAN. *(gives him a look)* You know who.

MICHAEL. *(yelling)* Oh no! Not Boot Camp Bertha? *(SUSAN just nods her head yes.)* Why didn't you tell me?

SUSAN. Because the last time I told you she was coming to visit, you disappeared for four days.

MICHAEL. You can't blame me. She'll have me marching up and down, remaking the beds, shining my shoes, polishing stuff….she thinks she's still in the army. If I leave now, I…..

SUSAN. Michael, don't even think about it.

MICHAEL. Oh, what am I going to do?

SUSAN. You'll survive.

*(The closet door opens and **KELLY** peers out. She sees **MICHAEL** and **SUSAN** and comes out with **PAUL**, now in male clothing.)*

MICHAEL. So does everything check out alright?

KELLY. Of course it does. Patrick has looked at the box and everything is fine.

SUSAN. Great, then you can start first thing in the morning.

PAUL. Kelly, I can't….

KELLY. Wait to get started, isn't that right Patrick?

PAUL. Whatever.

*(Enter **MURRAY** from the front entrance. **KELLY** who is standing at the entrance of the closet with **PAUL**, sees **MURRAY** first and quickly shoves **PAUL** back in the closet.)*

KELLY. He'll just double check it one last time, won't you Patrick?

PAUL. I will?

MURRAY. Hi everybody, it's looking a bit like rain. Just came back for my rain gear. *(exits to room 5 leaving the door open)*

SUSAN. Come on Michael we have things to do, we need to get a room ready for your sister.

MICHAEL. How about a pup tent in the yard?

(SUSAN and MICHAEL exit to the kitchen.)

MURRAY. *(reappears carrying a rain poncho)* Did I see Pauline bolt into the closet again?

KELLY. Yes, but she'll be right out.

PAUL. *(sticks his head out wearing the wig)* Actually, I think I'll stay in here a little while. I'm getting quite used to this room

MURRAY. Rock on dear, if that's what you want to do. Hopefully I'll see you at dinner. *(exits the front door)*

PAUL. *(steps out of the closet wearing the wig and men's clothing)* Kelly, I've had it. I want to go home. I don't even know who I'm supposed to be anymore. Look at me.

KELLY. I am looking at you, and you look cute with long hair.

PAUL. Kelly be serious. This is ridiculous.

(Enter SUSAN from the kitchen carrying towels. KELLY sees her and quickly whips the wig off of PAUL's head and throws it in the closet. SUSAN smiles at them, then heads upstage to the landing and, exits right.)

KELLY. Come on Patrick, I mean Paul. The Reverend is gone so you don't have to be Pauline, and Patrick isn't needed till tomorrow, so you get to be yourself right now. Come back to the room and I'll give your shoulders a little massage and you can start to relax. *(starts to pull him towards room six)*

PAUL. Kelly, I think you missed your calling.

KELLY. What do you mean?

PAUL. You could talk a penguin into living in the desert.

(They exit to room six closing the door.)

(Enter **MICHAEL** *from the office. He looks furtively around, then hurriedly crosses left to the closet. He enters the closet and reappears immediately carrying a suitcase. He closes the closet door with his back to the room as* **BERTHA** *enters from the front entrance.)*

*(***BERTHA***, age 50+, is a retired U.S. Army officer. She is dressed in either plain khaki pants or skirt, with flat shoes, and a modest short sleeve plain blouse. She wears little or no make-up, no jewelry except for a watch, and her hair is in a bun.)*

BERTHA. *(sees* **MICHAEL** *with his back to her)* TEN-HUT!

*(***MICHAEL*** immediately stands up straight and salutes holding the position, still with his back turned to* **BERTHA.***)*

ABOUT FACE!

*(***MICHAEL*** does a military style about face.)*

At ease, soldier.

MICHAEL. Bertha, give me a break would you? You're not in the army any more.

BERTHA. I know, but it's so much fun to see you jump. Now get over here. I suppose one hug would be permissible.

*(***BERTHA*** stiffly holds open her arms and takes a few steps into the room.* **MICHAEL** *holds out his arms and reluctantly steps towards* **BERTHA***. She inches a few steps further and* **MICHAEL** *moves closer until they meet in the middle an arms length apart. They both awkwardly attempt to hug the other person without having real contact. Finally,* **MICHAEL** *gives* **BERTHA** *a kiss on the cheek.)*

BERTHA. *(cont.)* *(quickly, pushes* **MICHAEL** *back)* Soldier, did you shave this morning?

MICHAEL. Of course I did.

BERTHA. Well next time, stand closer to the razor.

MICHAEL. Yes, sir.

BERTHA. Sir? Do I look like a Sir?

MICHAEL. Yes, Sir… I mean – no, ma'am – I mean – I don't know what I mean.

BERTHA. That's fifty soldier. *(MICHAEL just stares at her.)* NOW SOLDIER!

(MICHAEL drops to his knees and attempts to do a push up as SUSAN enters from upstage right.)

SUSAN. Oh Michael, what are you doing? Bertha, I'm so sorry, he must be in Stalag Seventeen again.

MICHAEL. Stalag Seventeen would have been a breeze compared to this nightmare. *(continues to attempt his second push-up)*

BERTHA. Hello Susan. Michael is just doing a few push-ups for me, aren't you soldier?

SUSAN. Well, I need him for the moment, so I'm sure you won't mind if he stops.

(MICHAEL stands up and kisses SUSAN.)

MICHAEL. Oh, thank you, thank you, thank you.

BERTHA. Public displays of affection are not necessary. Now Susan, where is my room?

SUSAN. You'll be in room four, down the hallway to the left.

BERTHA. I remember where it is, I'm not senile you know. I'll just go get my duffle bag from the car. *(exit front entrance)*

SUSAN. Well, she hasn't changed one bit.

MICHAEL. You're right. Do you remember the time when she had both you and Mary marching up and down the driveway on sentry duty?

SUSAN. Michael, Bertha has never made me march up and down the driveway.

MICHAEL. Oh, then who was it?

SUSAN. It certainly wasn't me.

MICHAEL. Maybe it was my other sister.

SUSAN. You haven't got another sister. Maybe it was Martha marching with Mary.

MICHAEL. Who's Martha?

SUSAN. Martha was your first wife dear.

MICHAEL. Oh yes, of course. *(pause)* Who's Mary?

SUSAN. Oh Malcolm, how am I supposed to know? You've never mentioned Mary before.

MICHAEL. I haven't?

SUSAN. No dear, so who's Mary?

MICHAEL. I don't know, who's Malcolm?

SUSAN. I don't know, maybe Malcolm is Mary's brother?

MICHAEL. Malcolm's sister was Mary? So it must have been Malcolm and Mary marching up and down with Bertha. Problem solved. Thanks dear.

SUSAN. You're welcome.

MICHAEL. Now, I think I'm going to hide on the back porch before Bertha has me doing K.P.

*(**SUSAN** exits to the office. **MICHAEL** is about to follow her as **BERTHA** enters from the front entrance carrying her duffle bag. He quickly ducks down below the counter. **BERTHA** heads upstage to the landing, as **MICHAEL** peeks up, He waits till she is just at the top of the steps, cups his hands around his mouth.)*

TEN HUT!

*(**BERTHA**, startled, drops the duffle bag on her foot, then falls to the ground with a loud yell. **MICHAEL** grins and runs into the office.)*

BERTHA. *(picks herself up, leaves the duffle bag where it is, and comes downstage)* Michael, you can run but you can't hide. *(exits to the office)*

PAUL. *(enters from room six, leaving the door open, calling over his shoulder)* I'll get your dress hon, it's still in the closet.

*(Moves downstage left to the closet and begins to enter as **BERTHA** re-enters from the office. She sees **PAUL** just outside the closet with his back to her.)*

BERTHA. ABOUT FACE!

PAUL. *(turns around)* What?

BERTHA. Sorry soldier, thought you were someone else. My name is Edwards, Captain Edwards, US Army retired. *(crosses left to shake hands)*

PAUL. Hello, I'm Pau....er... I mean...Patrick Harding. *(shakes hands)*

BERTHA. Nice to meet you Patrick, I'm Mr. Edward's sister. Why were you in the closet?

PAUL. Well, I was just getting...I mean...my girl...I mean...

BERTHA. Speak clearly, soldier!

PAUL. Well, I was just checking the electrical box.

BERTHA. And why would you be checking the electrical box?

PAUL. I'm supposed to wire the outside deck in the morning, and I'm not sure I know how to do it.

BERTHA. That's right up my alley. That was my outfit, Corps of Engineers. I'm a certified electrical G.S. zero eight five zero. Wiring is a piece of cake.

PAUL. Really?

BERTHA. I wouldn't lie to you, soldier. Now, when are you scheduled to do the work?

PAUL. Tomorrow morning.

BERTHA. You wouldn't mind a little help would you? It would feel good to be back in the saddle again.

PAUL. Not at all.

KELLY. *(enters from room six)* Paul, er – er Patrick, I thought you got lost.

PAUL. Kelly, let me introduce you to Ms. Edwards.

BERTHA. That's Captain Edwards to you young man. *(shakes hands with KELLY)*

PAUL. Captain Edwards is an electrical specialist and offered to help us with the wiring in the morning.

KELLY. That's terrific.

BERTHA. Reveille will be at O seven hundred and we should be finished by O nine hundred in time for breakfast.

KELLY. I sure hope breakfast is better than dinner.

BERTHA. And what's wrong with dinner, my sister-in-law is an excellent cook.

KELLY. Sure, if you enjoy roasted toad au jus with toad stool sauce.

BERTHA. Are they still pulling that fake menu stunt? I thought they'd given that up years ago. Don't worry about a thing, I'll take care of that.

PAUL. You will?

BERTHA. Are you hard of hearing boy?

KELLY. There, you see Patrick, everything is going to work out just fine, just like I told you it would.

PAUL. You mean, I don't have to eat that stuff?

BERTHA. *(to KELLY)* Is he a little slow or something? I'll see you both at nineteen hundred hours for dinner. *(exits upstage right with her duffle bag)*

PAUL. What's that in real time?

KELLY. I don't know but we can find out. Oh Paul, everything is working out perfectly for our romantic weekend. The electrical problem is solved, dinner is solved, and we have time before nineteen hundred hours, whenever that is, to just relax and enjoy each other. Nothing else can go wrong.

(Enter MURRAY from the front entrance wearing the poncho which appears to be wet. KELLY sees him and quickly pushes PAUL into the closet leaving the door ajar.)

MURRAY. Hi, Kelly.

KELLY. *(in a loud voice for PAUL's benefit)* Hi, Reverend. I see it's started to rain.

MURRAY. Just a little, but it looks like it's going to clear up. Has Pauline gone back into the closet again?

KELLY. Yes, you know…the claustrophobia therapy.

MURRAY. *(takes off the poncho, drapes it across the back of the rocking chair, picks up a magazine from the coffee table, then sits in the rocking chair)* Groovy, I expect she'll come out in a few minutes.

KELLY. You're staying here?

MURRAY. At least till it stops raining. *(starts to thumb through the magazine)*

KELLY. Wouldn't you be more comfortable in your room? Maybe a little nap before dinner?

MURRAY. Thanks for your concern, Kelly, but I'm not that ancient. I think I'll just wait here by the fire.

KELLY. Don't you have a sermon or something to work on? It would be quieter in your room.

MURRAY. Already taken care of right up here *(taps his forehead)*, and you and Pauline were my inspiration.

KELLY. We were?

MURRAY. Yep. While I was out on my walk I decided it's going to be on honesty and friendship.

KELLY. Reverend, may I ask you a direct question?

MURRAY. Rock on girl, but I strongly advise against it.

KELLY. Why?

MURRAY. It might provoke a direct answer.

KELLY. Oh dear, never mind. *(sticks her head in the closet)* Pauline?

PAUL. *(in a high voice from within the closet)* Now what, Kelly?

KELLY. It's time for you to come out of the closet.

PAUL. *(off)* Do I really have to?

KELLY. You can't stay in there all day.

PAUL. *(off)* Why not?

KELLY. We have things to do, remember?

(There is the sound of a balloon popping in the closet.)

PAUL. Well, OK.

*(Enters now wearing the wig and dress. The wig is crooked and **KELLY** quickly straightens it for him. He now has only one bosom. The left one is deflated. **PAUL** moves right behind the couch then as he turns left to face **MURRAY** quickly shoves the remaining balloon from the right side to the left, as **MURRAY** stands with his back to the fireplace.)*

PAUL. Hello again, Reverend.

MURRAY. Hi there, Pauline. Feeling better?

PAUL. Well, I'm starting to not like that closet.

KELLY. That's good because I think that's enough claustrophobia therapy for one day. Let's get back to our
room.

(The telephone rings. KELLY *quickly pushes* PAUL *into
the closet again as* SUSAN *enters from the kitchen and
picks up the phone.)*

Or maybe just one more session.

SUSAN. Cider Mill Inn. This is Ms. Edwards how can I help
you?

MURRAY. You're very enthusiastic about this therapy, Kelly,
but remember too much can do more harm than
good. Would you please excuse me for a moment.
(heads upstage and exits to the bathroom)

KELLY. *(to* PAUL *not heard by* SUSAN*)* Quick, get out of those
clothes and we can get to our room while he's in the
bathroom.

SUSAN.*(still on the telephone)* No, I'm sorry, we don't cur-
rently have a tradesman special running at this time....
Our next special will probably be in a few weeks.....
(looks around and smiles at KELLY*)* I'm thinking it will be
for Painters and Decorators.... Yes, dinner will still be
included.... Certainly, I'll can give you a call when we
run the ad. *(writes down a number)* Thank you for calling. *(hangs up as* PAUL *steps out of the closet minus the wig
and dress)* Well, all set for tomorrow?

PAUL. You bet, we've even got help.

SUSAN. Oh?

KELLY. Captain Edwards offered to work with us in the
morning. She says we'll be finished in time for breakfast.

SUSAN. Oh, OK, that sounds good. Just don't let my husband anywhere near anything electrical.

(The bathroom door starts to open as **SUSAN** *exits to the office.* **KELLY** *quickly shoves* **PAUL** *back in the closet.)*

MURRAY. *(enters from the bathroom, comes downstage and sits in the rocking chair)* Really Kelly, don't you think you're overdoing it with this closet therapy?

KELLY. You're probably right. *(puts her head in the closet)* Pauline, as soon as you're ready, we'll end this therapy session.

PAUL. Is that a promise?

KELLY. Cross my heart.

PAUL. Here we go again.

BERTHA. *(enters from upstage right)* Hello there, Ms. Harding.

KELLY. Hi...uh...uh...Captain Edwards. Have you met Reverend Robinson?

MURRAY. *(stands)* Hello. Did I hear Captain?

BERTHA. *(crosses left and shakes hands with* **MURRAY***)* U.S. Army, Corps of Engineers, retired, but please, call me Bertha. Nice to meet you padre.

MURRAY. Rock on, call me Murray. Please sit down.

(Sits in the rocking chair as **BERTHA** *sits on the couch left* **KELLY** *exits to the closet leaving the door ajar.)*

You must have led an interesting life, how long were you in the army?

BERTHA. Only twenty-two years. Picked up a piece of shrapnel and was forced to take a medical discharge. And you? How long have you been a padre?

MURRAY. All my life I guess, at least ever since my college days. "Make peace, not war" was my motto.

BERTHA. Well padre, that may be true, but without those of us in the service, peace wouldn't be possible.

MURRAY. Rock on Bertha. Live and let die. I guess we both found our calling. Never really wanted to do anything else, except ride my HOG.

BERTHA. That Harley outside is yours?

MURRAY. You bet your sweet bippie, it's my pride and joy.

MICHAEL. *(Appears from the office and stops just outside the door and cups his hands around his mouth.)*
TEN HUT!

*(**BERTHA** immediately jumps to her feet.)*
ABOUT FACE!

*(**BERTHA** does an about face. **MICHAEL** grins and gives her a little finger wave, then exits to the office.)*

BERTHA. *(takes two or three steps toward the counter)* I'm going to kill him.

MURRAY. *(laughing)* I don't think that would be a good idea.

BERTHA. I suppose not, after all he is my brother. Maybe I should learn to take it as well as dish it out.

MURRAY. That's the spirit. You know, when I'm upset I like to go for a ride…. Hey, how about you and me take a ride on the Harley?

BERTHA. That would be terrific, I haven't been on bike for …well, let's just say it's been a while.

MURRAY. Rock on. *(stands)* Hold on a few minutes while I check on the weather. Back in a jiffy. *(picks up his poncho and exits the front door)*

KELLY. *(who has been watching from the closet)* Paul…Now! *(**KELLY** steps out of the closet.)* Hi Ms. Edwards, I mean Captain. We're just making sure everything is ready for tomorrow morning. Come on out, Patrick.

BERTHA. You two don't need to worry about a thing. I have everything under control.

KELLY. Come on Patrick, let's go.

BERTHA. Does he always need to be told more than once? Mr. Harding get out here NOW!

PAUL. *(enters from the closet dressed as a man)* Hello, Captain.

*(**KELLY** grabs **PAUL**'s hand and begins to pull him upstage to the landing as **MURRAY** enters from the front entrance. **KELLY** sees him and quickly shoves **PAUL** into the bathroom and closes the door.)*

KELLY. You need to go, now.

(She turns and strikes a relaxed pose against the door.)

BERTHA. *(moves upstage toward* **KELLY***)* You missed your calling Ms. Harding. You would have done well in the army. Telling someone when they have to go to the bathroom, even I never did that. Good move, especially with someone so slow. *(claps her on the shoulder)*

*(***MICHAEL*** enters from the office, stops by the counter and cups his hands around his mouth.)*

(with her back to **MICHAEL***)* Hold it, soldier.

*(***MICHAEL*** freezes as ***BERTHA***, looking angry, turns and slowly comes downstage. When she gets to ***MICHAEL*** she gives him a big hug, as the bathroom door opens, ***KELLY*** realizing ***MURRAY*** is in danger of seeing ***PAUL*** quickly goes into the bathroom and closes the door.)*

MURRAY. *(who has been watching all this from the front entrance)* Rock on, Bertha! The weather's fine, the sun is out, let's hit the road. *(exit the front entrance)*

BERTHA. *(As she watches him leave, she pulls out her hair pin, shakes out her hair and hitches up her bosom.)* I can't wait to get my arms around you. Rock on, Padre!

(Exit the front door as **MICHAEL** *watches them leave. He rings the call bell several times, does a hop, skip and a jump as* **SUSAN** *enters from the office.)*

SUSAN. *(looks around)* Michael, did you ring the bell?

MICHAEL. Yes, Yes, Yes…My sister has gone for a ride with the Reverend, she even gave me a hug. No more Boot Camp Bertha.

SUSAN. I'm very happy for you dear. Now, can you just stay in reality for a little while? I have a few things I have to attend to.

MICHAEL. Oh, I don't know, I'm so happy I might just go visit Cleopatra at the Great Pyramid.

SUSAN. You know, Michael, sometimes I am a bit envious of your ability to get away like that. I wish I could do it.

MICHAEL. Oh you can, you can. Who would you like to be? Where would you like to go?

SUSAN. Well, I always thought if I was Queen Elizabeth the First of England, I might have married Sir Walter Raleigh.

MICHAEL. Oh, but you can't change history.

SUSAN. Oh, well, can I still be Elizabeth?

MICHAEL. Of course you can, dear. I'll be Francis Drake.

SUSAN. This sounds like fun. Now what do we do?

MICHAEL. I'm going to present myself to you at court, and you just take it from there. Now you sit on your throne my queen. *(leads her to the rocking chair and* **SUSAN** *sits)* Let the magic begin. (**MICHAEL** *does a sweeping bow.*) Your majesty.

SUSAN. So, you dare show yourself to me.

MICHAEL. I am your humble servant, madam.

SUSAN. What you are, is a no good privateer who has been raiding Spanish ships and have got me into me all sorts of trouble with the King of Spain.

*(***PAUL*** and ***KELLY*** peek out from the bathroom door and take a step or two towards bedroom six unseen by* **MICHAEL** *or* **SUSAN**.)

Do you find me to be a simpleton? You lied to me. I should have you beaten within an inch of your life. *(stands and grabs a poker iron and starts to brandish it about)*

PAUL. *(whispers to* **KELLY**) Kelly, she knows I lied. I don't want to be beaten. *(grabs* **KELLY** *and pulls her back into the bathroom and closes the door)*

SUSAN. *(begins to chase* **MICHAEL** *with the poker)* Take that you pirate.

MICHAEL. *(backing away)* There was never any violence in my fantasies. Susan, snap out of it.

SUSAN. Who's Susan? I'm Queen Elizabeth and you are my disloyal subject who is about to meet his maker. *(still chasing* **MICHAEL**)

MICHAEL. Susan, you must come back to me. This is only a flight of the imagination. Oh Lord, I've done it now. Please dear, you really don't want to do this.

SUSAN. You dare tell your Queen what to do?

(**PAUL** *and* **KELLY** *try once again to sneak back to their room as* **SUSAN** *brandishes her iron.*)

Arrest that man!

(**PAUL** *and* **KELLY** *duck back into the bathroom.*)

MICHAEL. But your majesty my ship is weighted down with treasure for you and England.

SUSAN. Treasure? Did you say treasure? How much?

MICHAEL. More than you have ever dreamed of.

SUSAN. Then I shall have to knight you. Kneel, Francis Drake.

(**MICHAEL** *manages, with great difficulty, to get down on one knee. She lays the poker on each of his shoulders.*)

Arise, Sir Francis Drake.

MICHAEL. I've kneeled and I can't get up.

SUSAN. Well, we command you to rise.

MICHAEL. I'll do my best my Queen. *(struggles to get up)*

SUSAN. So how do you feel SIR Francis Drake?

MICHAEL. My knees hurt.

SUSAN. Oh Michael, must you complain and ruin all the fun? Can we do it again?

MICHAEL. Only if it doesn't involve a poker iron and my knees. Oh, I'm so glad you're back my dear. *(gives her a hug)*

SUSAN. I don't know what you're talking about, I never left. Come on dear, let's go find your medicine. I really don't know why you were down on your knees to begin with, you know how bad that is for your arthritis. *(exits to the office)*

MICHAEL. I don't who I like better, the Queen or Susan. *(exits to the office)*

KELLY. *(opens the bathroom door)* You can come out now, they're gone. (**PAUL** *follows* **KELLY** *out of the bathroom.*)

PAUL. You heard her Kelly, she knows I lied. What are we going to do now?

KELLY. Give me a second to think. I know, maybe we tell her you're a nuclear power plant electrician, and you don't know anything about wiring up houses.

PAUL. Maybe we should just tell her the truth and beg for mercy?

KELLY. Oh Paul, we can still do this.

PAUL. Sure...and pigs can fly!

(**MICHAEL** *enters from the office.* **PAUL** *sees him and suddenly pulls* **KELLY** *into the bathroom with him and closes the door.* **MICHAEL** *creeps furtively downstage to the front entrance and looks out, then comes back, opens the closet door, looks in, closes the closet door, then crosses right to the counter and rings the bell and moves left a step or two.*)

SUSAN. *(enters from the kitchen)* What is it now dear?

MICHAEL. Come join me Gertie for the latest batch of hootch I just brewed.

SUSAN. Michael, you don't drink and my name isn't Gertie.

MICHAEL. Of course it isn't. *(grabs* **SUSAN** *by the arm and whispers)* We don't want anybody to think I drink, and we don't want anyone to know who you really are. It's a perfect cover for our underground brewery.

SUSAN. *(There is a long pause.)* Michael, what day is this?

MICHAEL. June 18, 1930.

SUSAN. Oh Lordy! It's prohibition and he's in the Promised Land Speakeasy again. Well, at least he's not Al Capone this time.

MICHAEL. Big Al will be here later, so keep your eye out, he'll know the password to get in.

SUSAN. As fun as it was dear, I just can't join you this time. I need a few moments to finish up Bertha's room.

MICHAEL. *(moves to the rocking chair)* I've even perfected how to take the tops off the bottles this time so there will be no more exploding beer bottles.

SUSAN. Oh Michael, I don't have time for this right now. You don't run an underground brewery, and you never invented anything.

MICHAEL. The secret of getting the top off the bottle is all in the technique.

SUSAN. If you say so dear. If you need me I'll be in Bertha's room. *(exit upstage right)*

KELLY. *(enters from the bathroom kissing **PAUL**)* Oh Paul, I should have joined you in the closet earlier.

MICHAEL. You just keep it slow and easy when you're taking the top off, it works like a charm.

PAUL. *(They pause on the landing.)* I beg your pardon?

KELLY. I'll decide when my top comes off, if it comes off.

MICHAEL. It used to be hard to get the tops off. I had to practice for quite a while, lots of trial and error before I got it right.

KELLY. *(comes downstage followed by **PAUL**)* You practiced taking tops off?

MICHAEL. Yes, the girls particularly like it when you do it for them.

PAUL. How many girls have you done this for?

MICHAEL. Oh, literally hundreds, they all appreciated it, but I do remember one time when I did it too quickly and one of the girls got really mad at me.

KELLY. Too much information, Mr. Edwards.

PAUL. I can't believe you're telling us this.

MICHAEL. Why not....better to tell you now so she doesn't get mad at you later when you take her top off.

KELLY. I told you I am the only one who decides when my top comes off.

PAUL. And I don't need lessons.

KELLY. *(giggling)* Really?

PAUL. Kelly! *(to* **MICHAEL***)* Any other advice for us?

MICHAEL. Well, you know the password you used to get into the Promised Land?

KELLY. There's a password?

MICHAEL. Of course, your boyfriend here would never have gotten this far without it.

PAUL. I can get pretty far without a password.

MICHAEL. Good boy, keeping it on the Q-T. Loose lips will get you into trouble.

KELLY. Oh, his lips can definitely get him into trouble.

PAUL. Kelly!

KELLY. Come on Paul, let's go practice as Mr. Edwards suggested. *(hand in hand she and* **PAUL** *move upstage towards bedroom six.)*

PAUL. I can't believe we just had this conversation, but at least we weren't talking about anything electrical.

KELLY. *(now outside the bedroom door)* There's enough electricity right here to worry about *(pauses)* …just as soon as you tell me the password.

PAUL. You've got to be kidding?

KELLY. The password please.

PAUL. I love you.

KELLY. *(opens the door)* Welcome to the Promised Land. *(They both exit and close the door.)*

*(***MICHAEL*** is still dozing in the rocking chair as* **JEAN** *and* **LARRY** *enter from the front door. They are wearing the identical clothes they had on in Act I, but* **JEAN** *is now carrying a briefcase. They move left and see* **MICHAEL***.)*

JEAN. Well, at least he's not in the closet this time.

(Sets down her briefcase, crosses left to **MICHAEL** *and waves her hand in front of his face.)*

MICHAEL. *(opens his eyes)* May I take your top off for you? *(He closes his eyes again.)*

JEAN. *(quickly backs away and crosses right to* **LARRY** *and pushes him towards* **MICHAEL***)* Larry, he wants to take my top off, do something.

LARRY. What do you want me to do, punch him in the nose?

JEAN. Of course not.

LARRY. Jean, he's just a crazy old man. You know I'm not sure this is a good idea.

JEAN. Of course it is. When they conned me into signing that work contract a few weeks ago I didn't think it was fair. You had to work when we were supposed to be on a vacation get-a-way.

LARRY. Jean, it's all water under the bridge now.

JEAN. Only a plumber would say that. I wasn't planning on doing anything until the paper I work for came up with that advertising scheme. It was just too perfect an opportunity to miss.

LARRY. You're going to end up getting us into trouble.

JEAN. You worry too much. There is nothing that can go wrong. We were wronged and now it's pay back time.

LARRY. That sounds rather mean spirited of you.

JEAN. I'd like to think of it as teaching them a lesson. After all, think of that poor young couple, Jenny and...

LARRY. Bobby.

JEAN. Right, they were conned too. We weren't the only ones. Besides, it's not like we're really taking advantage of them.

LARRY. Well, let's get this over with. *(looks around and sees* **MICHAEL** *still dozing)* I guess you'd better ring the bell. (**JEAN** *rings the bell.*)

MICHAEL. *(leaps to his feet)* It's a raid! That's the alarm, it's a raid. The cops are here. *(rushes up to the closet and opens the door)* Everybody, out the back door! *(He moves quickly left.)* Raid! Raid! Everybody out now! *(He pushes* **JEAN** *and* **LARRY** *left towards the closet.)* Hurry, hurry, the door will only hold 'em for a minute.

(SUSAN *comes running in from the office just in time to see* LARRY, JEAN, *and* MICHAEL *disappearing into the closet and closing the door. She rolls her eyes, crosses left and opens the closet door as* JEAN, LARRY, *and* MICHAEL *re-enter.*)

SUSAN. Mr. and Mrs. Hampton, what a surprise? We really didn't expect to see you again.

JEAN. I'm sure you didn't.

SUSAN. I do apologize for my husband's antics.

MICHAEL. I was only trying to keep them out of jail.

LARRY. *(whispers to* JEAN*)* Maybe he isn't so crazy after all. That just might be where we end up if you go through with this.

SUSAN. So what brings you back here?

JEAN. *(crosses right and picks up her briefcase)* I think we'd better sit down so I can explain.

(MICHAEL *stands with his back to the fire,* SUSAN *sits in the rocking chair,* JEAN *sits on the couch right and* LARRY *on the couch left.*)

Mrs. Edwards, my husband has something to say to you.

LARRY. What her husband has to say to you is that none of this was his idea. Jean, you're on your own.

JEAN. Very well. Mrs. Edwards, do you remember a few weeks ago receiving something in the mail from *[INSERT THE NAME OF A LOCAL NEWSPAPER]* ?

SUSAN. Oh yes, the survey, I completed it. How did you know?

JEAN. Well, I work for that newspaper.

SUSAN. And that's why you're here? Do I get my free half page of advertising?

JEAN. You certainly do, as a matter of fact it's running this weekend.

MICHAEL. You didn't tell me about this dear.

SUSAN. I wanted to surprise you.

MICHAEL. Well, you certainly did dear, wow, a half-page ad.

JEAN. *(takes a paper out of her briefcase)* Did you also fail to tell your husband about the free room you will be providing for any employees of the paper every weekend for an entire year?

SUSAN. I signed no such thing.

JEAN. I have your signature right here. It's all in the fine print. I believe it's in paragraph eleven.

SUSAN. Oh dear.

JEAN. We'd like you to show us to our room for the first of our many weekends together.

MICHAEL. I don't think that's going to happen, Mrs. Hampton.

JEAN. Oh and why not?

MICHAEL. Well, it's a long story, but the short of it is that a few years back Susan had a stroke and at the time was not capable of making any decisions. Power of attorney was vested in me, as well as sole title to the Cider Mill Inn. I'm afraid her signature on behalf of the Inn is simply not valid. But please, do thank your paper for the free advertisement.

JEAN. But, but...Larry, do something.

LARRY. Come on Jean, let's go. It's just not going to work. *(stands and heads to the front entrance)*

JEAN. *(puts the paper back in her briefcase and follows him)* Well how was I to know? And you weren't any help either.

LARRY. *(exits front entrance, followed by **JEAN**)* I know dear, but it's just as well.

SUSAN. *(stands and turns to **MICHAEL**)* Is that true dear?

MICHAEL. Is what true?

SUSAN. You know, what you just said?

MICHAEL. Well, *(He pauses and takes her hands in his.)* it really doesn't matter now, they're gone.

SUSAN. I love you, Michael.

MICHAEL. I love you, Susan.

(curtain)

FURNITURE AND PROPERTY LIST

ON STAGE
Reception counter ON IT: Telephone, bell BEHIND IT: Reservation forms – pink and yellow, pen, keys, calculator
Couch
Coffee table
Magazines
Vase of flowers
Rocking chair
Firewood bin

ACT I Scene One – OFFSTAGE
Toilet on a wheeled dolly (**MICHAEL**)
Union card (**LARRY**)
Two overnight bags (**LARRY**)
Bucket and plunger (**MICHAEL**)
Handkerchief (**JENNY**)
Suitcase (**BOBBY**)
Menu (**SUSAN**)

ACT I Scene Two – OFFSTAGE
Towels (**SUSAN**)
Overnight bag (**BILL**)
Purse with flask inside (**PENNY**)
Glass (**PENNY**)
Two suitcases (**JEFFREY**)
Set of plans (**MICHAEL**)
Overnight case (**JULIE**)
Tray with a wine glass, wine bottle and menu (**MICHAEL**)
Second wine bottle (**MICHAEL**)

ACT II – ONSTAGE
Basket of balloons

ACT II – OFFSTAGE
Large box (**SUSAN**)
Backpack (**PAUL**)
Overnight bag (**KELLY**)
Motorcycle helmet (**MURRAY**)
Menu (**MICHAEL**)
Man's pants, shirt, shoes (**KELLY** FOR **PAUL**)
Fire logs (**MICHAEL**)
Towels (**SUSAN**)
Suitcase in closet (**MICHAEL**)
Duffle bag (**BERTHA**)
Rain poncho (**MURRAY**)
Briefcase with contract (**JEAN**)

COSTUMES

MICHAEL
Blue jean overalls
Checkered shirts (2)
Work boots
Overcoat

JEAN
Sweater set
Pants
Sandals
Purse

BOBBY
T-shirt
Black jeans
Tennis shoes
Sandals

BILL
Long white shirt
Vest
Dress pants
Loafers
Glasses

PENNY
Casual summer dress
Sandals

PAUL
Blue jeans
T-shirt
Baseball cap
Tennis shoes
Padded bosom
Dress
Women's shoes

MURRY
Black leather outfit
Motor cycle helmet
Clerical collar
Grey shirt
Dark dress pants
Black shoes

PERSONAL
Recorder (**BILL**)
Wallet with Union card (**PAUL**)
Union card (**LARRY**)

SUSAN
Long skirt
Blouse
Flat shoes
Plain dress

LARRY
Short sleeve shirt
Khaki pants
Casual shoes

JENNY
Casual skirt
Blouse or Top
Purse

JEFFREY
Tan Polo shirt
Brown Pants
Brown shoes

JULIE
Low cut blouse
Short skirt
High heels
Fashionable hat
Purse
Sun glasses

KELLY
Summer dress
Sandals
Wig or hair extension

BERTHA
Khaki pants or skirt
Plain Blouse
Flat shoes

WHAT IS SUSAN'S SECRET?

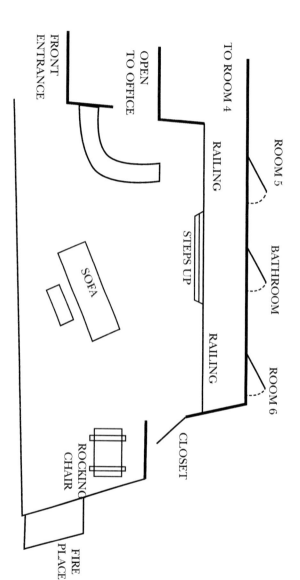

Set design courtesy of the Author

THE CIDER MILL INN

ROOM 5

BATHROOM

ROOM 6

CLOSET

TO ROOM 4

FRONT
ENTRANCE

OPEN
TO OFFICE

RAILING

STEPS UP

RAILING

SOFA

ROCKING
CHAIR

FIRE
PLACE

Works by
Michael Parker...

The Amorous Ambassador

Hotbed Hotel

The Lone Star Love Potion

Never Kiss a Naughty Nanny

The Sensuous Senator

There's a Burglar in My Bed

Who's in Bed with the Butler

Whose Wives Are They Anyway?

(with Susan Parker)

Sex Please We're Sixty!

Sin, Sex, and the C.I.A.

What is Susan's Secret?

Please visit our website **samuelfrench.com** for complete
descriptions and licensing information.

OTHER TITLES AVAILABLE FROM SAMUEL FRENCH

SIN, SEX & THE C.I.A.

Michael Parker and Susan Parker

Comedy / 3m, 4f

Huge oil reserves have been discovered in The Chagos Islands. O.P.E.C. is pressuring the Chagosians to join the cartel. A C.I.A. agent and an under Secretary of State, whose life appears to be run by her libido, are sent to a C.I.A. safe house in the mountains of Virginia to begin negotiations for the U.S. to place the Chagos Islands under their protection. Unfortunately, no one knows who the islands' representative really is. We are left to wonder how the C.I.A. agent ever got the job. He gets caught in all his own booby traps, he electrocutes himself, he sets fire to himself, he gets a bucket stuck on his head, and finally locks himself in his own handcuffs! Add to the inevitable chaos, a stranded televangelist, his innocent secretary (or is she?), an ex-marine caretaker, who isn't what he seems to be, and a mysterious, glamorous neighbor, and you have a complex, laugh out loud farce, that can be played on any stage.

"This play has character development, as every good play must."
"The plot has more turns than Soda Bay Road."
– *Record Bee,* Lakeport, California

"*Sin, Sex & the C.I.A.* generously incorporates every aspect of farcical comedy into its insanely funny script."
– Hemet, California

"Packed with double entendres and lot of humor"
"….comic moments and hearty laughs."
– *Sarasota Herald Tribune,* Sarasota, Florida

"Nearly every element of comic farce is present in this show – for an audience that means laughter from beginning to end!"
– Paradise Playhouse, Excelsior Springs, MO

"Laugh out loud hilarity…the laughs are relentless."
– *The Press-enterprise,* California

"Rib splittingly funny"
"A complex and hilariously funny plot"
"The Parkers are masters at this style of theatre"
– *Englewood Sun Herald,* Englewood, Florida

OTHER TITLES AVAILABLE FROM SAMUEL FRENCH

SEX PLEASE, WE'RE SIXTY!

Michael Parker and Susan Parker

Farce / 2m, 4f

Mrs. Stancliffe's Rose Cottage Bed & Breakfast has been successful for many years. Her guests (nearly all women) return year after year. Her next door neighbor, the elderly, silver-tongued, Bud "Bud the Stud" Davis believes they come to spend time with him in romantic liaisons. The prim and proper Mrs. Stancliffe steadfastly denies this, but really doesn't do anything to prevent it. She reluctantly accepts the fact that "Bud the Stud" is, in fact, good for business. Her other neighbor and would-be suitor Henry Mitchell is a retired chemist who has developed a blue pill called "Venusia," after Venus the goddess of love, to increase the libido of menopausal women. The pill has not been tested. Add to the guest list three older women: Victoria Ambrose, a romance novelist whose personal life seems to be lacking in romance; Hillary Hudson, a friend of Henry's who has agreed to test the Venusia: and Charmaine Beauregard, a "Southern Belle" whose libido does not need to be increased! Bud gets his hands on some of the Venusia pills and the fun begins, as he attempts to entertain all three women! The women mix up Bud's Viagra pills with the Venusia, and we soon discover that it has a strange effect on men: it gives them all the symptoms of menopausal women, complete with hot flashes, mood swings, weeping and irritability! When the mayhem settles down, all the women find their lives moving in new and surprising directions.

"This play is a winner."
- Rocky Varcoe. Owner & CEO Class Act Dinner Theatre,
Toronto, Canada

"Fast paced and hilarious."
- *The Californian*

SAMUEL FRENCH STAFF

Nate Collins
President

Ken Dingledine
Director of Operations,
Vice President

Bruce Lazarus
Executive Director,
General Counsel

Rita Maté
Director of Finance

ACCOUNTING

Lori Thimsen | Director of Licensing Compliance
Nehal Kumar | Senior Accounting Associate
Charles Graytok | Accounting and Finance Manager
Glenn Halcomb | Royalty Administration
Jessica Zheng | Accounts Receivable
Andy Lian | Accounts Payable
Charlie Sou | Accounting Associate
Joann Mannello | Orders Administrator

BUSINESS AFFAIRS

Caitlin Bartow | Assistant to the Executive Director

CORPORATE COMMUNICATIONS

Abbie Van Nostrand | Director of Corporate
                         Communications

CUSTOMER SERVICE AND LICENSING

Laura Lindson | Licensing Services Manager
Kim Rogers | Theatrical Specialist
Matthew Akers | Theatrical Specialist
Ashley Byrne | Theatrical Specialist
Jennifer Carter | Theatrical Specialist
Annette Storckman | Theatrical Specialist
Julia Izumi | Theatrical Specialist
Sarah Weber | Theatrical Specialist
Nicholas Dawson | Theatrical Specialist
David Kimple | Theatrical Specialist
Ryan McLeod | Theatrical Specialist
Carly Erickson | Theatrical Specialist

EDITORIAL

Amy Rose Marsh | Literary Manager
Ben Coleman | Literary Associate

MARKETING

Ryan Pointer | Marketing Manager
Courtney Kochuba | Marketing Associate
Chris Kam | Marketing Associate

PUBLICATIONS AND PRODUCT DEVELOPMENT

David Geer | Publications Manager
Tyler Mullen | Publications Associate
Emily Sorensen | Publications Associate
Derek P. Hassler | Musical Products Coordinator
Zachary Orts | Musical Materials Coordinator

OPERATIONS

Casey McLain | Operations Supervisor
Elizabeth Minski | Office Coordinator, Reception
Coryn Carson | Office Coordinator, Reception

SAMUEL FRENCH BOOKSHOP (LOS ANGELES)

Joyce Mehess | Bookstore Manager
Cory DeLair | Bookstore Buyer
Kristen Springer | Customer Service Manager
Tim Coultas | Bookstore Associate
Bryan Jansyn | Bookstore Associate
Alfred Contreras | Shipping & Receiving

LONDON OFFICE

Anne-Marie Ashman | Accounts Assistant
Felicity Barks | Rights & Contracts Associate
Steve Blacker | Bookshop Associate
David Bray | Customer Services Associate
Robert Cooke | Assistant Buyer
Stephanie Dawson | Amateur Licensing Associate
Simon Ellison | Retail Sales Manager
Robert Hamilton | Amateur Licensing Associate
Peter Langdon | Marketing Manager
Louise Mappley | Amateur Licensing Associate
James Nicolau | Despatch Associate
Emma Anacootee-Parmar | Production/Editorial
                            Controller
Martin Phillips | Librarian
Panos Panayi | Company Accountant
Zubayed Rahman | Despatch Associate
Steve Sanderson | Royalty Administration Supervisor
Douglas Schatz | Acting Executive Director
Roger Sheppard | I.T. Manager
Debbie Simmons | Licensing Sales Team Leader
Peter Smith | Amateur Licensing Associate
Garry Spratley | Customer Service Manager
David Webster | UK Operations Director
Sarah Wolf | Rights Director